Only God Can Judge

Revised Edition

Reginald Val Davin

Only
God
Can
Judge

Revised Edition

Reginald Val Davin

ARPress
45 Dan Road Suite 5
Canton MA 02021

Hotline: 1(888) 821-0229
Fax: 1(508) 545-7580

Ordering Information:
Quantity sales. Special discounts are available on quantity purchases by corporations, associations, and others. For details, contact the publisher at the address above.

Printed in the United States of America.

ISBN-13:   Paperback   979-8-89389-250-5
            eBook   979-8-89676-600-1

Library of Congress Control Number: 2024925997

Contents

About the Author

Reginald Val Davin is a 70-year-old native of New York City. He attended Herbert H. Lehman University in New York and received a bachelor's degree in English. He also graduated from Columbia College in Chicago, Illinois. A school that specializes in helping students develop their creative writing skills.

Mr. Davin is President and Founder of Gumbo & Associates, a nonprofit organization in Los Angeles California with a "Base Prevention Program" to keep young men and women out of prison by helping them to acquire critical thinking skills with the game of chess. This technique is designed to teach the participants how to make "good decisions" by applying the principals of a chess game to become successful in whatever type of career they choose to pursue.

Mr. Davin believes this type of curriculum is greatly needed in the urban community to provide alternatives for young people who desperately need to change their lives. This book was written with the idea of using the profits from book sales to be used by Gumbo & Associates, so that the organization will continue to remain an important "tool" in helping to reduce "recidivism" in the urban community.

Acknowledgements

I would like to thank the following people for their unselfish contributions with assisting me in writing this book: My daughter, Ursel, for her support with helping me to write this novel; My two "best" friends, Mercedes and Ethan, for believing in me and providing the financial support to complete the manuscript: Mr. Lloyd Outten, for his belief in my project and assisting me with the capital to make sure this novel would be finished; And most of all, "My Creator," All Mighty God, for giving me the faith to believe that this book was meant to be written. Last, but certainly not least, to the many people reading this book and contributing their support with helping me to keep young men and women out of prison! Thank you all.

ONE

ROSEMARY PATRICIA SHUMSKY was a 49-year-old Superior Court Judge in New York City at the criminal court building in downtown Manhattan. She was dressed in a black robe and pacing the carpeted floor of her chambers in a pair of white tennis shoes. On the desk was a picture of Rosemary and Robert Shumsky on their wedding day 27 years ago. Beside the photograph was a gold framed picture of their son, Thomas, wearing a white karate suit with a black belt and the same tennis shoes on Rosemary Shumsky's feet! There was a knock at the door.

"Come in," she said.

A middle-aged black woman in a sleeveless cotton dress opened the door. "Mr. Shumsky is here to see you, Your Honor," said the secretary.

"Send him in," said Rosemary sighing with relief.

The secretary closed the door. A few moments later, a handsome Caucasian of 51 entered the chambers wearing a policeman's uniform with three stripes on both sleeves and a 38 revolver on his right hip. The 5 foot 8-inch male had short red hair, strawberry mustache, and black shoes. The Sergeant closed the door, removed his hat, and stared at his wife. There was a strange expression on her face as if she was frightened about something. The Sergeant wanted to say how much he missed her during their three-week separation but was hoping she would mention it first.

"You left word at the station you wanted to see me right away," he said tucking his hat under his arm like a cadet. "What's going on?"

"I know this is going to sound crazy, but I'm not who you think I am," she said walking towards him.

"What do you mean?"

"I mean I'm not your wife even though I look like my mother."

"Well, if you're not my wife, who are you then?"

"I'm your son, Thomas!" she said standing in front of him.

"I don't know what kind of game you're trying to play, but it isn't funny," he said putting on his hat.

"I'm not playing any games, dad. I'm really your son," she insisted.

"Listen Rosemary, our son is dead and neither one of us can bring him back," he said angrily, "and you need to stop thinking he's still alive because he isn't."

"BUT I'M NOT DEAD!" she screamed at the top of her lungs. "And I'll tell you something else. David Cross knows mom's real name is Fatima Muttalib and that both of you are wanted for murder by the Arab Government for killing two Muslim Soldiers!"

"How did he find out about me and your mother?"

"From his father, Phillip Cross, who works for the Department of Immigration."

Robert Shumsky knew it was impossible for Thomas to be alive again and believed his wife was suffering from a mental breakdown, due to their son being shot in his apartment by Detective David Cross. "I know it's hard to accept what's happened, but you've got to pull yourself together," he said holding his wife by the shoulders.

Rosemary looked around the chambers in search of a way to prove she was telling the truth and quickly snatched the revolver from his holster. "Put your hands up," she said pressing the barrel against his chest.

"Are you crazy, give me my gun," he said grabbing the revolver.

Rosemary gave the Sergeant a karate chop across his wrist, causing him to release the barrel, and then kicked him in the stomach like a martial arts expert. The Sergeant bent forward like he had been hit with a medicine ball and staggered backwards. The

135-pound magistrate walked to her desk with the gun in her hand. Before she could put the 38 next to the picture of Thomas in his karate suit, she was tackled around the waist from behind by the Sergeant. His hat fell. Rosemary also hit the floor like a quarterback being sacked. The revolver in her hand landed beside the hat as they crashed on the carpet together. The magistrate skillfully elbowed him across the face with her left arm. He immediately unwrapped his arms from around her waist and began holding his nose. Blood dripped from his nostrils like a broken water faucet. Rosemary swiftly rolled over and sat on the Sergeant's chest to keep him pinned down. He immediately punched the right side of her rib cage with all his strength. Rosemary toppled over on the floor like a cowboy in a saloon fight. Before the Sergeant could hit her again, Rosemary laughed.

"You remember asking me to show you what I learned in my karate class, and we had a fight on the patio after you called me a sissy?" she said breathing heavily.

The Sergeant wiped the blood from his nose with the back of his hand. The bleeding had stopped. His body ached unbearably. He stood up on his feet and stared at his wife, realizing she was really his son because no one else was on the patio that morning but him and Thomas! Rosemary held out her hand, so the Sergeant could pull her up off the carpet. She threw her arms around his waist and rested her head on his chest.

"I'm sorry I had to kick you like I did on the patio that morning, but I didn't know what else to do," she said panting.

TWO

ROBERT BERNARD SHUMSKY was baffled, befuddled, and bewildered. Thomas was alive again by some unexplainable miracle. The question now was, where was his mother? Would she continue to be Thomas for the rest of her life or just take his place momentarily?

Rosemary lifted her head from the Sergeant's chest. "What are we going to do, Dad? I can't continue to be inside my mother's body for the rest of my life."

"I guess we'll just have to figure it out, but I'm wondering if God had something to do with you coming back as your mother."

Rosemary took a step backwards. "Now why would God want me to come back as my own mother?"

"I don't know, but if you have a better explanation, I'd like to hear it. There's a reason why all of this is happening, and we've just got to figure it out."

The Sergeant walked to the desk and recovered his hat and revolver off the floor. On one side of the chambers were shelves of law books on the wall. On the opposite side of the room was the office door. In front of the desk was a brown leather couch against the wall and the bathroom door a few feet away from the couch. Rosemary went to the couch and sat down. There was a box on the couch with the clothes Thomas wore the day he was killed. The Sergeant placed his hat beside the box as he sat on the couch alongside Rosemary.

"I wish I could have been the kind of policeman you wanted me to be, but I just wasn't cut out to be like you and my grandfather," she said sadly.

"What are you talking about, you were a good cop."

"Dad, you know that isn't true. No one wants his son to be a homosexual! And I know David Cross was the one who started those rumors about me being gay and the reason you broke his jaw."

The Sergeant fell back against the seat. "You're right," he said frowning. "I should have tried to protect you a long time ago, but I was just hoping that after you became a policeman, it would make you more masculine."

"Dad, being gay isn't a matter of choice. I was born this way."

"I still believe people can change themselves if they want to, Thomas," he sighed.

"How come you and mom are wanted by the Arab Government?"

"Two Muslim Soldiers tried to arrest me and my sister, and Fatima shot both of them after they killed Rosemary. Then she used a fake passport to come to America as my sister because the Arabs were looking for us. I didn't think anyone knew her real name was Fatima Muttalib until you said David found out from his father."

"Why would they still be looking for you, when this happened a long time ago?"

"Because there's no statute of limitations on murder in Arabia. Which reminds me, David Cross said in his report that he shot Frederick Steinberg because Frederick was trying to take his gun away from him and it went off while you stood at the apartment door."

"That's a lie," she stated angrily. "I heard a gunshot as I was opening the door and saw Freddy lying on the floor. I was going to the bedroom to use the telephone and call an ambulance, and that's when David shot me."

"So, you weren't shot at the door like his report said?"

"Yeah, Freddy can tell you what happened. All he had was a shoulder wound."

"Frederick Steinberg is dead, Tommy! He was shot twice in the chest and his family is asking the district attorney's office for an investigation, but there're no witnesses to refute David's report. And why did he shoot the both of you anyway?"

"Because we had proof that his father was making immigrants pay him money to stay in the country."

"What kind of proof?

"Pictures of David receiving payoffs from the migrants, as well as everyone willing to testify about them being blackmailed. Freddy kept the pictures in a shoebox with a lot of other stuff we had in the apartment."

"Whatever was in the apartment is gone, Tommy. David got rid of everything before he wrote that phony report. What did Freddy do with the pictures?"

"He told me he was going to give them to his father."

"How did you find out Phillip Cross was blackmailing people?"

"I went to a party with David and his father at a gay club and met a drag queen named Trixie. She told me they were blackmailing a man named, Muhammad. After I told Freddy what Trixie said, he suggested we go undercover and get proof Muhammad was being extorted."

"Wait a minute, what were David and his father doing at a gay club?"

"Because they're both bisexual!" she said as if it was apparent. "They were in the backroom smoking marijuana and drinking alcohol with some other gay people when I got there."

The Sergeant folded his arms together as if he was listening to a soap opera.

"Not only that," continued Rosemary, "the transvestite who owns the club has known Phillip and his son for years because they helped her get a passport to come to New York."

"Phillip helped me get your mother a birth certificate when

she first arrived, but I didn't think he was in the business of blackmailing people."

"And David began helping him after he became a policeman."

The Sergeant looked at Rosemary's feet. "The last time I saw those shoes you're wearing; they were at the coroner's office. How did you get them back?"

"They must have come out of that box right beside your hat, but I don't remember putting them on before you came,"

There was a knock at the door.

The secretary poked her head inside the chambers. "Detective Cross is here to see you, Your Honor."

"Tell him to wait," said Rosemary quickly.

The secretary closed the door. Rosemary looked at the Sergeant. "Dad, I want you to hide in the bathroom while I talk to David," she suggested. "He's going think I'm a real judge and might say something to help us prove his report is a lie."

"Good idea," he agreed rising from the couch, "but take off those shoes, so he won't get suspicious about why you have them on."

The Sergeant walked into the bathroom, closed the door, and kept his ear pinned to the wall.

Rosemary strolled to the desk, sat in the chair, and pressed the button on the intercom. "You can send Mr. Cross in," she said kicking both shoes off under the desk.

All at once, Rosemary felt dizzy. She tried to shake off the drowsiness, but suddenly lost consciousness as if she had been under hypnosis and fell forward in the chair with her forehead propped on top of the desk.

THREE

FATIMA AMINA MUTTALIB was born on August 12, 1917. She was raised in a city 282-miles northeast of Mecca called Medina. Her mother, Aisha, was also born in Medina. Fatima's father, Omar, was born in Mecca and grew up in a town, 54-miles southeast of Mecca known as Ta'if. Omar was a traveling salesman and sold prayer rugs, Kufi Caps, and prayer oil in many of the cities across the country to earn a living. Omar also taught Fatima how to read and write English, so she could help him sell the merchandise to many of the tourists visiting Saudi Arabia. When Fatima was 14 years old, Omar told her about a certain type of spirit which had been part of the Muttalib's family for 5 generations and called a *Ruh*!

"What is a *Ruh*?" she asked.

"It is a dead person's spirit, and it will come back to life if someone in our family is murdered."

"How does it come back to life?"

"After someone is murdered, the *Ruh* attaches itself to the person's shoes and when another family member puts on the shoes, they become the dead person who was killed."

Fatima sat behind her father on a camel traveling to Mecca. She was attired in a black hijab, black scarf around her head, and black veil across the face. Omar wore a white kufi cap and full-length dashiki. He was of medium height, 45-years-old, and possessed an olive complexion with no facial hair. Aisha was an attractive dark-haired woman of 42. She was dressed exactly like her daughter and sitting on a second camel, while pulling a third humped back animal by the reins loaded with the merchandise her husband sold, and leather sandals she handcrafted together with a sewing needle.

"But let me say this," continued Omar, "both the dead person and the family member who puts on the shoes must be born in the same month and on the same day. After the killer is brought to justice, the spirit will return back to the person who was murdered."

"Has this ever happened to you?"

Omar gazed at the evening sun setting behind the hills of desert sand. "Only once," he said sadly. "My twin brother, Ali, witnessed a murder and was killed by the same person he saw murder someone else. After I put on Ali's sandals, I found out how he actually died."

"What happened?"

"Two men, one named Malik and other named Al Jabbar, were arguing inside Malik's tent. Al Jabbar pulled out his knife and attempted to back out of the tent but suddenly lost his balance and fell on his own knife. Ali went inside the tent just in time to see Malik standing over Al Jabbar's body. Malik claimed Al Jabbar stabbed himself. Ali went to see if he was dead and that is when Malik stabbed Ali."

"So, Malik stabbed your brother because he thought Ali would not believe Al Jabbar stabbed himself accidently?"

"Exactly."

"What were they arguing about?"

"Both of them worked for a rich widow named Miriam Akbar. She told them she was looking for her long-lost brother and would pay five thousand dirhams to anyone that found him. After Al Jabbar learned where her brother was, he decided not to share the reward with Malik, which is why they were arguing in the tent."

"How did Miriam get separated from her brother?"

"She belonged to a tribe in Abyssinia called the Habesha. Her tribe had a battle with the Persian Empire. The Habesha people were slaughtered but the women and children were held captive, along with Miriam's little brother who was just three months old. The Persians sold Miriam's brother to my brother in a trade for money and Ali gave him the name Mustafa because it means, The Chosen One."

"How did Miriam expect to find her brother, when he was just a baby?"

"Miriam and Mustafa had the same birthmark on their necks, and she showed Malik and Al Jabbar where the birthmark was. Al Jabbar met Ali and Mustafa on his way to Antioch and saw the birthmark on Mustafa's neck. He told Ali about Miriam searching for her brother but did not tell Mustafa because he wanted to surprise him about his sister being rich."

"How did she become rich?"

"She ran away from the Persian tribe and went to live in the City of Ta'if where I grew up and became a prostitute and belly dancer. Ta'if has always been known as a place where women were not treated like slaves by men."

The sun had finally set behind the horizon. Omar pulled the reins on his camel and stopped. He looked over his shoulder at his daughter. "I will finish the story tomorrow, but right now it is time to eat," he said dismounting.

After setting up camp, the Muttalib family ate their evening meal and went to sleep so they could get an early start to the Holy City of Mecca in time to celebrate the month of Ramadan.

FOUR

THE MUTTALIB FAMILY continued on their journey to Mecca the next morning. Once again Fatima sat on the back of the camel with arms around her father's waist. "So, finish telling me the story please," she said yawning.

"Miriam and the other dancers lived in a boarding house owned by my old friend Abu Bakr. When Miriam was nineteen-years old, she met a rich old man from Antioch and got married, but he died from leprosy and left her with his estate in Antioch. After Al Jabbar and Malik started working for Miriam, is when she offered them a reward to find her brother."

"What happened after your brother was killed?"

"My father told me to put on Ali's sandals to find out the truth because Malik claimed Ali tried to break up the fight and was stabbed by Al Jabbar."

"So, Malik tried to say Al Jabbar killed your brother?"

"Yes, and there no way to prove otherwise, until I scraped Malik's skin from under Ali's fingernails to show they were wrestling before Ali was stabbed, which showed how Malik got the scar on his cheek."

"You mean Ali scratched Malik's face just before he was killed?"

"Yes, and Malik confessed about stabbing my brother after I told him what actually happened."

"So, the sandals helped you find out the truth?"

"No, the spirit did," he corrected her. "The sandals were just something it used to bring Ali's murderer to justice, although no one in our family knows what makes the *Ruh* work the way it does."

"What happened to Mustafa?"

"Ali told him to wait outside while he went into the tent. Mustafa heard Ali and Malik arguing and looked inside. After seeing that Ali had been stabbed, he took off running. I heard he went to Jerusalem and was living with a rich king, but I was never able to find him after he ran away."

"Will this stuff about spirits coming back to life ever happen to me?" she said timidly.

"I do not know my darling," he said noticing Mount Hira, where Prophet Muhammad received his first revelation from God through the Angel Gabriel, "but if it does you will know why."

F I V E

DETECTIVE DAVID CROSS entered Judge Shumsky's chambers and closed the door. He was decorated in a beige suit, striped tie, and stood 6 feet tall. There were blond eyebrows over his blue eyes. His broad shoulders made him look like he wore shoulder pads beneath his jacket. On his feet were cordovan shoes. He noticed the judge slumped over in her chair and rushed to the desk.

"Mrs. Shumsky," he said pulling her back against the chair.

Rosemary opened her eyes and stared at the detective wondering how long she had been asleep. She noticed the scar on his cheek. She also became aware of his hand on her shoulder. "What are you doing here?" she said pushing his hand away.

David Cross stepped backwards and put both hands into his pants pockets. "I came to say how sorry I am about your son being killed and how much of a good cop Thomas was," he said trying to sound sincere. "You probably know I was the one who shot Frederick Steinberg after Frederick shot your son."

"What was Frederick doing with a gun, he is a fireman."

"Actually, the gun was mine," he admitted. "I was arresting Frederick when Thomas walked into the apartment. Frederick tried to take my gun and it went off and killed Thomas as he stood by the door. I managed to shoot Frederick several times while we were still wrestling with the gun and your son was on the floor by the door."

"So, Frederick never meant to shoot my son, he was just trying to take the gun away from you?"

"Something like that. It's all in the report I wrote."

"How did you get that scar on your face?"

David Cross removed the right hand from his pocket and messaged the scab on his cheekbone. "I got it while fighting with Frederick," he said quickly, "but I didn't come here just to talk about Thomas, I also came to talk to you."

"What do you mean?"

David Cross put his hand back in his pocket. "The District Attorney's Office wants to hold a hearing in your courtroom because Frederick's father claims I shot his son in cold blood and that Frederick had evidence my father was making immigrants pay money to stay in the United States."

"No one has told me about a hearing," she said leaning back against the chair. "When did you come by this information?"

"I have my ways," he said smartly. "So, when it does, I want you to transfer the case to Judge Raymond's courtroom."

Rosemary looked at the detective as if he had just escaped from a mental institution. "First of all, Mr. Cross, let's get one thing clear. I do not take orders from you or Judge Raymond and if there is a hearing in my courtroom, you can rest assure I will preside over it."

Detective Cross took both hands out of his pockets and folded his arms together. "Well let me make myself clear," he said as if he was a presiding judge. "Your name isn't Rosemary Shumsky. It's Fatima Muttalib. I found that out when you asked my father to help you get out of Saudi Arabia and into the United States with Thomas about ten years ago."

Rosemary watched the brash detective stick out his chest like he had the upper hand.

"Now if the hearing is transferred to Raymond's courtroom, no one will know that you and your husband are wanted by the Arab Government for murder. But if it isn't transferred, then both of will be extradited back to Arabia to stand trial, which I'm sure you wouldn't want to happen."

David Cross waited for a response from the 5 foot 5-inch

magistrate with long black hair, but she seemed shell shocked after being told to cooperate or be deported back to her country for manslaughter. The young sleuth put both hands into his pants pockets again as if he didn't want to seem like a bully.

"You've known Frederick Steinberg ever since he went to high school with your son, so what chance have I got to win a hearing in your courtroom?" he said regretfully.

Rosemary kept silent.

"If I were you, ma'am, I would just transfer everything to Raymond's court room and let this investigation be done with. Frederick and Thomas are dead, and nothing can bring either one of them back."

Rosemary wondered what she was going to do as David Cross walked out of the office and closed the door behind him.

SIX

THE KING OF SAUDI ARABIA saw Fatima Muttalib at the Jumu'ah Prayer Service and sent word to her father about paying a handsome price for his daughter's hand in marriage. Omar was overjoyed about the proposal and arranged for Fatima to marry someone old enough to be her grandfather! King Lahore Ibn Azad had two wives. They gave him children, but no sons. The marriage to Fatima was to provide him with a male offspring to carry on the family name. The King offered to give Omar camels and sheep as a down payment during the month of Ramadan. The wedding was to be held in the Royal Palace after the completion of Ramadan and the balance paid as soon as the ceremony was over. The contract was written on a scroll as proof of the agreement.

Omar was elated. Now he could settle down and not have to travel all over the desert to earn a living. He also believed Fatima would be pleased, knowing her social status would be raised to a position of admiration and respect with being married to King Azad. Omar rushed home to tell his wife and daughter what he thought would be good news. The Muttalib Family was camped in a tent on the outskirts of Mecca during the month of Ramadan. Aisha was clothed in a long black dress and a white apron around her waist. She was cooking lamb and waiting for the sun to set so the family could break the fast and eat together. Fatima was dressed in the same style of clothing as her mother and sitting on the dirt floor with her legs crossed and reading the Holy Quran.

Omar was attired in his kufi cap, dashiki, and baggy pants. He entered the tent and kicked off his sandals. "All praises are due to Allah," he said looking at Fatima. "King Azad has asked me for your hand in marriage, with an offer of money and livestock if I gave him my consent. The wedding date will be set after Ramadan is over and he wants to give me a few camels and sheep before you are married."

Aisha wiped her hands on the apron and dropped to her knees in front of Fatima. "You are going to be the wife of the greatest king in Saudi Arabia," she said excited. "All praises are due to Allah."

Fatima stared at Omar as he stood behind Aisha grinning with pride. "How does this king know I am the right person to marry?" said Fatima unenthused.

The question caught Omar completely off guard. "Are you not pleased about this arrangement? I thought you would be happy."

Fatima slammed the book of Islamic scriptures closed. "No, I am not pleased," she said boldly.

"Do not talk to your father that way, Amina," intruded Aisha. "Your father works hard to provide for us, and this is how you talk to him?"

Fatima began to feel uncomfortable as she looked at her father. She didn't mind marrying someone that was rich, but not somebody she'd never met before.

Omar sat beside Fatima and crossed his legs. "Why are you not pleased? I thought this would make you happy, but I see it does not. So, tell me what you have to say."

"She is just a child, Omar," insisted Aisha, sitting beside her husband. "Many years from now she will realize it was the right thing to do."

Omar placed his arm around Aisha's shoulder. "Let my daughter speak," he said calmly. "She has a right to say what is on her mind because everyone has a voice in this family."

"The Holy Quran says to honor and respect your parents, so if both of you want me to get married, then I will do it," she said sorrowfully. "But the Quran also says that Allah will judge us by our intentions. So, is this arrangement intended for my happiness, or for yours?"

"HOW DARE YOU SAY SUCH A THING, AMINA?" bellowed Aisha, breaking away from Omar's arm. "WE WANT YOU TO BE HAPPY."

"Actually, I want all of us to be happy," added Omar.

"You cannot buy happiness, Father. Would you want me to marry someone who is rich? Or someone like you, who makes me and my mother happy even though he is not a king?"

Omar placed his arm around Aisha again. "Our daughter has the wisdom of men twice her age. You are right. No father should force his daughter to marry someone she does not love. I will tell King Azad to dissolve the contract because my daughter does not wish to get married just yet. And besides, she is too young anyway."

"Wait a minute, you agreed to this marriage in a contract?" asked Fatima alarmed.

"Yes, but I believe King Azad is a man of understanding," assured Omar. "I am sure he will consider the fact that I forgot to consider my daughter's feelings."

"I hope you are right," said Fatima hoping King Azad would allow her father to go back on his word.

SEVEN

THE SERGEANT FLEW out of the bathroom like a bat out of hell. "If that son of a bitch thinks he's going to get away with blackmailing you and me, I've got a big surprise for him when I get back to the station," he said boiling with anger.

"Robert, what are you doing here?" said Rosemary startled, "and why were you in the bathroom?"

"What do you mean, I've been here for over an hour."

"When did you get here?" she said, walking towards him.

The Sergeant noticed his wife wasn't wearing any shoes. "What a minute, are you Thomas or Rosemary?" he said confused.

"What are you talking about?"

"When I first got here, you were wearing tennis shoes and pretending to be Thomas. Now you're acting like his mother again."

Rosemary suddenly remembered the story about a person's spirit coming back to life through their shoes. "Where are the shoes you said I was wearing?"

"I don't know, but you had them on just before David Cross came to see you."

Rosemary walked back to the chair and stared at her son's shoes underneath the desk. She recalled putting them on but couldn't remember anything after that. She looked at the Sergeant. "What did Thomas say while I was wearing his shoes?" she asked, remembering they were born on the same day in August.

"That David Cross shot him, and it wasn't accidental like his report said. You want to tell me what the hell is going on around here, Rosemary? Or Thomas, or whoever you are."

Rosemary sat on the couch, realizing her son was back from the dead! "I need for you to sit down so I can tell you why Thomas might be alive again."

"Before you do that, I want to know why you left the country with Thomas about ten years ago like David Cross said."

"I went to Antioch because I received word my father was ill."

"Why didn't you tell me when you got back? And where was I anyway?"

"You were in the hospital," she said agitated. "And I did not tell you because you were too busy being a celebrity, after you got your picture in the newspaper for capturing two bank robbers."

The Sergeant frowned. "Yeah, I did get a little bigheaded after I got that medal for bravery from the Mayor," he admitted.

"You have been a little bigheaded about a lot of things, Robert. Especially when I tried to tell you our son was different from other children when he was born."

"So, what are you trying to say, that Thomas was born to be some kind of freak?"

"That is exactly what I'm saying," she said frankly, "and he is not some kind of freak like you and everybody else thinks he is. Thomas is our son and only God has the right to judge him, just like it says in the Bible."

"The Bible, since when did you start believing in the Bible?"

"When I realized my cousin, Mustafa, was telling me the truth about gay people and I didn't want to listen. We were arguing about him being a homosexual, because he said he was a eunuch and used to work for a King in Jerusalem.

"I thought eunuchs were people who've been castrated?"

"The word eunuch does mean that, but Mustafa said he had not been castrated when he works for the king and that some gay people would still go to Heaven according to the Bible. So, I read the Book of Isaiah, and it was true.

"Let me get this straight," he said as if his wife was under arrest. "I knew Mustafa was gay, because we met in Antioch before my sister was killed, but now you're saying he believes being gay doesn't matter because the Bible says so?"

"No, he did not say it exactly like that," she said wishing Mustafa were there to defend himself. "He said God is the only one who knows if being gay is right or wrong and no one has the right to judge other people, except Allah."

The chambers became deftly quiet while they both stared at each other.

Rosemary started talking again. "And he said that if I had a gay son, I would not be so quick to condemn homosexuals, and he was right. I once believed that being gay was a matter of choice, but now I know better because I tried to change my own son and it did not work."

The Sergeant walked to the couch but didn't sit down. "Whether a person chooses to be a homosexual or not, the Bible also says they were punished in the story of Sodom and Gomorrah, so let's not forget about that," he reminded her.

"Yes, I know because it says the same thing the Holy Quran," she said sadly, "but he reminded me about my obligation as a Muslim to seek knowledge from the time I am born, until the day I die. So, I read the Book of Isaiah, and it was true about eunuchs going to Heaven."

The Sergeant sat on the couch and placed an arm around his wife's shoulder. "Everyone has the right to be whatever they want to be, but it sounds like your cousin became a eunuch because he was already gay. And from the way you talk, it seems like he didn't have to be either one."

Rosemary jumped to her feet. "Are you saying my son wanted to be gay?"

The Sergeant looked at the box of clothes Thomas wore when

he was killed. "You know only he can answer that."

"Oh really," she said knowing her husband was trying to evade the question. "Thomas did everything possible to be like you and now he is dead because of you!"

"Because of me!?" he exclaimed, rising to his feet. "I loved Thomas."

"But not enough to try and understand him," she rebutted. "You never let me raise him as a mother and you never took the time to really be his father. All you cared about was catching criminals and being in the newspapers."

"Listen, Fatima, I tried. . ."

"NO, YOU LISTEN DAMMIT," she interrupted. "I wanted to be a good wife, even though I was a prostitute, but all you wanted from me were children. My father believed all women should have a voice in family matters and not be treated like slaves!"

The Sergeant massaged the back of his neck. "You're right about me not taking the time to understand Thomas, and I told him this morning about how sorry I was for not being the kind of father I should've been."

A moment of silence hung in the air as Robert Shumsky massaged his eyeballs. "And you're right about me not allowing you to be the type of mother he probably needed," he said after pausing. "You're a Muslim and we just have different ways of looking at things because I'm Jewish. I know I should've listened to you a long time ago, and I'm really sorry I didn't."

The Sergeant grabbed his hat from off the couch and walked to the door. Rosemary grabbed his arm before he could leave. "Listen, Robert, we both made a lot of mistakes," she said squeezing his arm." But now it is time to help our son prove David Cross is a murderer. Maybe after that, we can pick up where we left off and start over."

"The Sergeant wanted to smile, but self-pity was written all across his face. "So, where do we start?" he said, tossing his hat on the couch. "No one is going to believe Thomas is alive when his body is still at the morgue."

Rosemary noticed the blood on his uniform. "How did you get those stains on your shirt?"

"I got it from fighting with you after you turned into Thomas. He grabbed my gun and when I tried to take it back, he elbowed me across the face."

"Does it still hurt?"

"Hell yeah. Thomas really knows his stuff."

Rosemary gently kissed the Sergeant's nose and then unbuttoned her robe and began undressing. A few minutes later, she was completely nude and looked like a mannequin without clothes in a store window. Her breasts were firm and sensual. She put the box of clothes and his hat on the floor and lay on the couch with her legs spread apart. The Sergeant started taking off his clothes as fast as he could and looked like someone on the cover of a body building magazine as he removed his underwear. He rushed to the couch, dropped to his knees, and began massaging Rosemary's clitoris with his tongue.

"Faster, Robert, faster. . ." she begged.

He began moving his head up and down like pistons in a car engine. Rosemary opened her legs as wide as she could. Her body quivered with excitement. The judge's chambers was completely quiet, except for the sound of Rosemary moaning with pleasure.

All at once, she lifted herself upon the elbows, grabbed the Sergeant's head, and began grinding her body against his mouth. A few moments later, she erupted like a volcano full of lava and fell backwards on the couch. Robert Shumsky climbed on top of her body. Rosemary threw her arms around his neck and roped her legs around his waist like they were in a wrestling match. Their bodies became connected. He kissed every part of her face. Rosemary could feel the intensity building inside her husband and held on as tightly as she could. Without warning, every circuit from the top of his head to the bottom of his feet became overloaded as if he was about to blow a fuse. Robert Shumsky came to a climax and exploded like cannon balls during the Civil War between the North and South. There was only the sound of his heart pounding inside his chest as if he were out of breath. The Sergeant laid his head on his wife's soft breasts. He felt exhausted. Rosemary also felt drained. She dropped her legs from around his waist and released his neck. From the first time Robert Shumsky and Fatima Muttalib began making love, they both knew there was something special about their relationship when it came to satisfying each other. Aside from the fact they were never really in love with one another, seems to make the chemistry between them just that much more enjoyable.

"We must help our son bring David Cross to justice, so that Tommy's soul will be able to rest," she whispered into his ear.

The Sergeant lifted his head. "What do you mean?"

Rosemary never dreamed she would become someone that was dead after putting on their shoes, as she explained to her husband why their son had been reincarnated through a spirit which had been with her family for generations and called a "Ruh."

EIGHT

"OMAR MUTTALIB, ARE YOU INSIDE YOUR TENT?" exclaimed a loud voice.

Omar poked his head from out of the tent and came face to face with a husky Arab Soldier wearing a silver helmet, armored breast plate, and boots made from goat skin. The soldier was seated on a black stallion with a scroll in his right hand and a steel sword hanging from his belt.

"Are you Omar Muttalib?"

"I am he."

"King Lahore Ibn Azad has ordered me to give you this message," he said handing Omar the scroll.

Omar stepped outside without sandals to receive a scroll rolled up like a diploma and tied with a string. After giving Omar the document, he yanked the reins on the horse's mouth. The Arabian thoroughbred reared up on its hind legs and galloped away. Omar returned inside the tent. Aisha and Fatima were sitting on the dirt floor waiting for Omar to read what was written on the parchment. Omar untied the string and read the message out loud.

"In The name of Allah, Most Gracious, Most Merciful. King Lahore Ibn Azad greets you, Omar Muttalib, with the hope and prayer that Allah will accept your fast during this Holy Month of Ramadan. He also would like to extend his gratitude and appreciation for accepting an agreement to marry your daughter, Fatima Muttalib, this ninth month, and fifteenth day of Ramadan."

Omar stopped to take a breath. Something in his heart told him King Lahore Ibn Azad expected those he formed agreements with, not go back on their word once a contract was written.

"King Lahore now looks forward to receiving the date you will offer your daughter's hand in marriage after the month of Ramadan is completed," continued Omar. "The Royal Family will also attend this ceremony as witnesses to this momentous occasion. May Allah continue to bestow His blessing upon you, Omar Muttalib, and your family forever. King Lahore Ibn Azad."

The aroma of lamb permeated the room but didn't arouse anyone's appetite after Omar read what was on the scroll. Fatima sensed her father was worried. King Azad was reminding him with a written document to ensure the wedding would go as planned. Omar rolled the scroll back together and tied it with the string. Fatima was right, he thought. The King had his heart set on getting married. Omar knew if he tried to back out of the agreement, King Azad would be extremely upset, not to mention embarrassed. King Lahore Ibn Azad was no ordinary monarch and would probably have him imprisoned for trying to breach a contract which included money and livestock as part of the negotiations.

Aisha broke the silence first. "What are you going to do, Omar?" she said anxiously. "Azad expects you to keep your word. And if you do not, you will be taken away by an angry king and Fatima will be his wife anyway."

Fatima rose from the floor, walked over to her father, and put her arms around his waist. "Do not worry, I will marry him," she said resting her head on his chest. "It is better I get married, then you be punished."

Omar grabbed her shoulders. "You will do no such thing," he said bravely. "I will not allow you to be unhappy because Azad is looking out for his own interest."

"But Father, what about. . ."

Omar placed a finger over Fatima's lips before she could finish talking. "Azad is not God, Fatima, he is just a king. I will think of something to make sure your happiness comes first."

"What will you do?"

"I do not know but let us eat and give praises to Allah for giving me a daughter such as you," he said releasing her shoulders.

NINE

OMAR MUTTALIB shook his head with satisfaction. Once again, Aisha had cooked a delicious leg of lamb. "I have made my decision," he stated licking his fingertips. "I will tell the king I cannot agree to the contract because my daughter wishes to marry someone of her own choice."

"But he will put you in a prison camp, Omar!" said Aisha dreadfully.

"Yes, he might," agreed Omar, "but if he is someone who understands that no one should be forced to do something against their will, then all will be well."

"And if he does not understand, what then?" quarreled Aisha.

"Then whatever happens will be the will of Allah."

"But Father, would it not be better if . . ."

"No buts, Fatima. I want you and your mother to go to Ta'if and stay with my old friend, Abu Bakr. He will watch over you and Aisha if something does happen to me."

"I won't go," insisted Aisha. "Let Fatima go. My place is with you."

"Aisha be reasonable. Things could be dangerous."

"You want me to be reasonable, but you won't do the same," she remarked. "What will become of your daughter and me if King Azad makes you a slave?"

Omar looked at Aisha, knowing she wasn't going to change her mind. "Very well, Fatima will go alone. Let us get ready, so we can go to Abu Bakr's tent and tell him what happened. That way she will be able to leave tonight with him under the cover of darkness."

TEN

ABU BAKR was a slender man of 71, with a long white beard, and stood 5 feet 7 inches tall. He looked 20 years younger, due to his two youthful wives and 7 children being a fountain of rejuvenation from which he drank to keep his ageless appearance. Abu Bakr had no brothers or sisters and was born in Cairo Egypt. His father, Abu Sufyan, was a doctor who never went to medical school, but learned to perform surgeries, deliver babies, and cure common ailments from watching other physicians operate on their patients. After getting married, Abu Sufyan moved to the Town of Ta'if and taught his only child everything he knew about medicine before he died. However, Abu Bakr decided to be a real estate agent instead of following in his father's footsteps and was now retired with property he obtained twenty-five years ago in Ta'if, where he lived with both spouses in separate homes. He also possessed a harem of single women living in a private residence he owned on the outskirts of town. The females were belly dancers and prostitutes and paid some of their earnings to him to live in the housing complex.

Abu Bakr was in Mecca during the month of Ramadan and happened to meet Omar Muttalib on the tenth day of Ramadan. After arriving at Abu Bakr's tent on the night Omar wanted Fatima to depart from Mecca, he told Abu Bakr why he needed his daughter to leave as soon as possible. Abu Bakr took Fatima to Ta'if and then returned to Mecca to complete the Fast of Ramadan, as well as find out whether King Azad would allow Omar to dissolve the same contract of marriage to Fatima that had been agreed upon.

ELEVEN

FATIMA RESIDED in a large tent with Abu Bakr's first wife because her children were females. She was dressed in a housecoat and standing outside the tent with a towel around her neck, pouring water from a vase over her scalp to wash away the soap from her hair, when her attention was overtaken by Abu Bakr's voice.

"Your mother and father are in King Azad's prison camp," he said regretfully.

Fatima turned around. Abu Bakr looked extremely depressed, she thought. Fatima wrapped her head with the towel. "I must go to Mecca," she said walking towards the tent.

Abu Bakr grabbed her arm. Fatima tried to break free. "Let me go," she demanded.

"You cannot go, Fatima," he said holding her tightly. "King Azad will still force you to marry him and keep your mother and father in his prison camp anyway. And your father instructed me to never let you come to Mecca to save him. Ever!"

Fatima threw herself into Abu Bakr's arms and wailed like women do over the death of a relative. Abu Bakr rested his chin on top of her head. "If only I had the money, I could buy back their freedom."

Fatima raised her head. "What do you mean?" she said wiping her snotty nose.

"He wants your father to give him the same amount of money that was agreed upon in the contract before Omar went back on his word."

"How much was it?"

"Ten thousand dirhams!"

Fatima pushed herself away from Abu Bakr. "That is not true," she said furiously. "It was much less than that."

"I know, but Azad wants to teach your father a lesson for embarrassing him."

"I want you to help me get the money," she said with both hands on her hips.

"Help you how?"

"I will be like the women here, who sell themselves for money."

"You will do no such thing," he said flatly. "Your father would never allow you to become a common whore for his sake."

"Would you prefer I do nothing and let them be slaves in a prison camp for the rest of their lives?"

"No, I do not, but two wrongs do not make a right. And prostitution is not the way to save your mother and father."

"My father once told me about a woman who came here to make money and married someone that was very rich. Maybe the same will happen to me."

Abu Bakr chuckled. "That is true," he acknowledged. "Her name was Miriam Akbar. I remember when she first came to Ta'if and how different she was from all the other girls. But you and Mariam are not the same, Fatima. She knew how to dance and could charm the pants off those who watched her perform."

"Then I will learn to dance," said Fatima stubbornly.

Abu Bakr shook his head. "Your mother and father would never like the idea of you to becoming a belly dancer," he said with a sigh, "but get dressed and I will let you talk to some of the other girls who dance for their customers."

TWELVE

ABU BAKR INTRODUCED FATIMA to the other dancers as, Sarah, just in case King Azad was searching for Fatima's whereabouts. Everyone in the housing complex liked Fatima immediately because of her charming and outgoing personality. Fatima not only mastered the art of dancing to the rhythm of instruments, she also became skilled with using a tambourine when performing in front of an audience. Not long after she began doing private shows for customers, did she convince the other dancers to form a group and charge admission. The sixteen females agreed. They were known as the "Ta'if Dancers." Sasha Bin Amir came up with the idea of using a pole when performing, after noticing a rope hanging down from the top of the tent where the audience sat. Everyone thought the whole concept would be exciting to the male spectators and put a thick 8-foot pole made from bamboo in the middle of the tent during their performances. However, Fatima was the star of the show because of the way she used her acrobatic agility to dazzle everyone watching her.

Two years later, customers paid extra dirhams to get front row seats. The ensemble's popularity spread like a sandstorm. The number of women increased to 25 exotic dancers, many of whom came from every part of the Arabian Desert in search of stardom and money. Abu Bakr's life also changed, after it was agreed upon by the dancers that he be hired as manager and provide them with protection both inside the tent and around the housing complex.

Fatima was now a celebrity at the delicate age of sixteen. Men threw money at her feet every evening. She was also handsomely paid for services she rendered to those who could afford to pay for sexual favors when the show was over. Several months after Fatima's sixteenth birthday, Abu Bakr had acquired enough money from his real estate business to pay for Omar and Aisha's release from prison. However, Fatima insisted she pay for her parents' freedom because it was the honorable thing to do. Abu Bakr was very pleased she hadn't lost her sense of integrity like many people who start acquiring money. Five years after Omar and Aisha Muttalib were imprisoned, Fatima had saved more than enough dirhams to pay for their release.

THIRTEEN

"I HAVE THE MONEY!" said Fatima happily.

Abu Bakr was outside his tent wearing silk clothes and talking to his wife. He turned around. "I always knew this day would come," he grinned. "You are a child destined for even greater things to happen in your life."

Fatima was draped in a black satin hijab and silver slippers. "When can we take this money to the king?"

"In two days. I will make arrangements, but you must stay here."

"But I wish to go with you."

"That would not be wise," he asserted with caution. "King Azad is someone who does not forget easily. I will take the money to him and bring your family here. Trust my judgement, Fatima. All of you will soon be together again. Of this I am sure."

"SARAH!" YELLED THE WOMAN. "COME QUICKLY!"

Fatima and Abu Bakr stared at the Ta'if Dancer racing towards them. She was without shoes and adorned in a housecoat.

"Sasha has been bitten by a snake at the boarding house where we live!" she said gasping for breath.

"Where was she bitten?" inquired Abu Bakr.

"On her foot, about five minutes ago."

Abu Bakr ran inside his tent and returned with a double-edged sword. "Let us go," he said with urgency.

Fatima jumped on the back of a camel. The young show girl mounted herself on the same camel and held Fatima around the waist. Abu Bakr leaped upon another four-legged mammal. The humpbacks hurriedly galloped down the road. After reaching the boarding house, the three of them rushed into a room filled with the other tenants circling around Sasha's bed. Curtains were used as a door to separate each compartment. Sasha was lying on her back. Her right leg was swollen from the ankle to the knee cap. A strip of leather was tied around her right thigh to keep the poison from spreading throughout the body.

"I want everyone to leave," said Abu Bakr with authority.

The dancers walked out of the room, one by one. Fatima remained by the bed.

Abu Bakr looked at Fatima. "I do not want you to see this," he said holding the double edge sword, "and close the curtain behind you."

Fatima glanced at the sword as she exited the compartment. Sasha suddenly screamed at the top of her lungs. Fatima wanted to return but knew better than to disobey Abu Bakr's orders. Sasha kept screaming as if the surgery was unbearable. Fatima ran outside the boarding house to avoid hearing Sasha continuously squeal from the harrowing pain of her leg being amputated.

FOURTEEN

THE SUN WAS NO LONGER VISIBLE. The evening sky was filled with stars. The air was humid. The town was quiet. There was a full moon shining down on the district like a spotlight inside a movie theater. The Ta'if Dancers were sleeping in their compartments. Fatima was sitting on a sand hill just outside the boarding house thinking about Sasha Bin Amir. What was Sasha going to do, Fatima wondered? Sasha was sure to live a life of poverty, now that she could not dance anymore and had no other occupational skills. Fatima began thinking about the type of life she was living and believed her father would be overcome with shame if he knew she was just a common whore. And what did she intend to do once her mother and father's freedom were paid for? Get married to someone that was not as rich as King Azad and have a family? Who would want to marry a prostitute that dances?

"Why are you not sleeping?" said Abu Bakr.

Fatima turned around. Abu Bakr's clothes were stained with blood. He appeared extremely tired as he lay on a bed of sand next to Fatima.

"How is she doing?"

"Not good. I gave her something for the pain, but she has another pain I cannot stop."

"What do you mean?"

"She came to Ta'if to try and make enough money to bring her mother and two brother here, but now she talks of suicide."

"Suicide!" said Fatima surprised.

"Yes, you gave her hope before all of this happened. In fact, you gave many people here, including myself, a reason to think about the future. You have no idea how much you are admired by those whose lives you have changed. Your parents would not be ashamed of what you did to buy their freedom."

Fatima suddenly felt rejuvenated upon hearing Abu Bakr's words. "I cannot let Sasha lose hope," she said standing up. "I will give her the money, so she can be with the rest of her family."

"But what about your family?"

"I will make more money. I have more ideas."

FIFTEEN

FATIMA GAVE SASHA 10,000 dirhams. Abu Bakr made crutches out of wood for Sasha to walk with. Sasha was immensely grateful for the money and sent word to her mother and both brothers that she would pay the cost to whoever brought them from Damascus to Ta'if. Sasha continued helping Fatima by becoming a choreographer for the Ta'if Dancers. Fatima had Abu Bakr build a larger tent for a bigger audience and hired musicians to play music while they danced, as well as having the musicians teach some of the other girls how to play the instruments. Once again, the Ta'if Dancers became the topic of conversation throughout the entire district on the east coast of the Red Sea.

Sasha's family came to Ta'if with all their possessions. Sasha's mother was a frail woman of 64 with silver grey hair. The teenage brothers were both undernourished but still overjoyed to be with their big sister again. Sasha introduced her relatives to Fatima as Sarah, since no one knew Fatima's name was changed by Abu Bakr. Fatima was happy she could help bring Sasha and her family together. Especially after seeing how poor they were.

The person who brought Sasha's family from Damascus was a 22-year-old merchant named Bilal. He was a handsome Arab and possessed a charming voice to go along with his extensive vocabulary. After paying Bilal the money, Sasha invited him to see the Ta'if Dancers perform without charging admission. He was greatly impressed with how each dancer used the 8-foot pole along with the music and decided to remain after the show to talk to the teenage starlet named Sarah about going on the road. Sarah and Bilal were inside the theater alone and sitting on a Persian rug which covered the sand inside the tent from one side to the other.

It was well past midnight. The sun was due to rise within a few hours.

"You should really consider traveling to other cities," he suggested. "With a group like this, all of you would definitely make a lot of money."

On the rug in front of Bilal was a goblet carved from glass and a silver vase containing liquor. Bilal poured himself a drink while sitting with his legs crossed. He was donned in silk clothes and leather sandals. Around his waist hung a belt with a pouch to hold his money. It was apparent he made a suitable profit from his occupation as a guide traveling across the desert.

"We could never go to other cities," she responded modestly. "And besides, it would take more money than we have to travel from one place to another."

Bilal drank the wine in one gulp. "Suppose I could arrange for you to travel alone, would you be interested?" he asked, putting the empty goblet beside him.

Sarah wore a red brassiere and G-string panties. Her stomach was bare. Around the waist was a fishnet skirt, allowing her underwear to be visible. There were bracelets with bells around each ankle, toenails coated with red enamel to match her lipstick, and black hair falling to the shoulders.

"No, I would not," she laughed. "When I am with the other girls, I feel like we are a family. And anyway, who would take me to these different places?"

"I would," he offered. "I know a king in Jerusalem that would pay you fifty dinars every night to dance for him."

"How do you know he would pay so much?"

"Because I was one of his servants when I lived there."

"What kind of servant?"

"You do not want to know what kind of employee I was, my little dancer," he said pouring another drink. "Let us just say I know he would pay well to be entertained by you."

"Why would I not want to know what you did for the king when you lived there?"

"Because you are too young to understand certain things about life."

"Try me," she said folding her arms together.

Once again Bilal swallowed the alcohol in one gulp, with a decision to tell her about his retirement from an old occupation he had as a servant for the king. "I used to be a eunuch when I lived with King Fulk in Jerusalem. Do you know what a eunuch is?"

"No, what is it?"

"Someone who takes care of the king's concubines. However, many people think eunuchs are people who have to be castrated before they can work inside the king's harem."

Sarah's eyes became as large as two silver dollars. "Why would you let yourself be castrated?" she said, unfolding her arms.

"I have not had my testicles removed physically, but the king used me to watch over his concubines because he knew I did not like having sex with them. However, there are men who have actually been castrated."

"So, you've never had sex with a woman your whole life?" she said believing such a thing was impossible.

"I did not say that," he said cleverly. "I do have sex, but it is with men not women."

Bilal could see the wheels turning inside Sarah's head. He was also feeling the effects of having drank the liquor too quickly. "What is the matter?"

"I was thinking about the Quran and that Allah destroyed Sodom and Gomorrah because men were having sex with each other."

"Do you know what the Bible says about eunuchs?" he asked, rocking from side to side.

"No, I do not," she answered, noticing he was a little tipsy." The

Bible does not contain the whole truth anymore and the reason I do not read it."

"Are not the Muslims supposed to seek knowledge from the cradle to the grave?" he challenged.

"Yes, but there are many things in the Bible that have been changed," she countered.

"I was hoping you would be more understanding, since the type of life you live is not something Allah would approve of either," he remarked as though she had forgotten about the speck in her own eye."

Sarah remained quiet, knowing Bilal made a good point.

"I really wonder what you would do if your son became attracted to another man? I am certain you would feel differently than you do now."

"That would never happen because I would teach him that being attracted to another man is something he can control."

"One day, Sarah, you will discover that isn't true. And hopefully you will take time out to read what the Bible says."

"The Book of Allah is all I need."

"Well just remember it says in Isaiah, chapter fifty-six, verses four and five, that Allah said; To the eunuch who keeps My Sabbath, and chooses what pleases Me, and hold fast My covenant, even them will I give My house and within My walls a place and a name better than that of the sons and daughters."

"My child will never be attracted to men, so I do not have to worry about what the Book of Isaiah says."

"Where are you from, Sarah?" he said leaning back on his elbows. "I have been to Ta'if many times but have never seen you before."

"I was born in Medina and came here a few years ago with a friend of my father named Abu Bakr."

"I've never met Abu Bakr personally, but I know he is well

respected amongst the old merchants and has helped a lot of people start their own businesses."

"And he helped my father, and his brother become tradesmen while they all lived together in Ta'if, but my uncle was murdered by some crazy man named Malik, and my father started working alone."

"What was your uncle's name?" he said immediately.

"Ali Muttalib."

"Your uncle was my father!" he said, staring at Sarah as if she was a ghost. "I mean, Ali adopted me when I three months old and was murdered when I was twelve."

"Why do you go by the name Bilal? My father said your name was Mustafa."

"After Ali was killed, I changed it just in case Malik decided to look for me too. But let me ask you the same question. Ali said your name was Fatima. Why does everyone call you Sarah?

Fatima told Mustafa what happened to her parents, why Abu Bakr changed her name, and why she became a dancer. Then she told him about his rich sister living in Antioch and searching for her long-lost brother with a reward for anyone who found him.

"I think we should go to Antioch and see if your sister will give me enough money to pay for my parents' freedom," she proposed. "I heard that she is very rich, which means you will be rich too."

"Well, my little cousin, any plan to help me become wealthy like you say is definitely worth undertaking," he said with bloodshot pupils.

"Good, we will go as soon as I pack my clothes."

Fatima told Abu Bakr that Bilal, whose real name was Mustafa, was Miriam Akbar's long-lost brother, and she was taking him to Antioch to collect the reward for finding him, with the hope it would be enough to pay for her family's imprisonment. She also told the other dancers she was going away on business and would be back as soon as she could.

SIXTEEN

ROSEMARY and the Sergeant were reclining on the couch with her head resting against his chest. His arm was around her shoulder. They were completely nude. The time was 9:05 a.m.

"Your father wearing his brother's sandals is the same thing that's happening to you," he said, understanding why his son was reincarnated, "but who's going to believe he's alive because of some tennis shoes?"

"The only person who needs to be convinced is David," she said rising from the couch to get dressed.

"David knows Thomas died in the apartment, so what's going to make him think any differently?" he said retrieving his underwear from off the floor.

Rosemary adjusted her brassiere. "Did you know David has a scar on his cheek?"

"I saw it when I talked to him about his report," he said tucking his tee-shirt into his undershorts, "but what does it matter?"

Rosemary fastened the top button of her black robe. "He said he got it from fighting with Frederick, but Frederick used to bite his fingernails all the time. So, the skin from David's face could be under our son's fingernails."

The Sergeant snapped his finger. "Just like it was under Ali's fingernails when Malik stabbed him. Thomas did say he was standing next to David when he got shot. Maybe he did scratch his face before he fell."

"I want you to go to the coroner's office and find out for sure and get photographs of Frederick's hands to show he does not have fingernails."

The Sergeant put on his socks and shoes wondering if his wife had a plan. "What's going to make David believe Thomas is alive again?"

"If Thomas makes David's father thinks he's alive, then Phillip will tell his son."

The Sergeant strapped his holster around the waist. "Why should Thomas make Phillip think he isn't dead instead of David?"

"Because David will wonder how his father knows everything when David, Thomas, and Frederick were the only ones in the apartment," she said walking to the desk and sitting down. "If Phillip believes his son is guilty of murder, he is going to get a lawyer. Then we can put pressure on David to come clean and think about a plea bargain."

"What do we do about David trying to blackmail you because he knows the Arab Government is looking for us?"

Rosemary folded her hands together. "There is nothing we can do," she replied sounding defenseless. "If the U.S. Government finds out I am a fugitive from justice and became a superior court judge, they are going to be very embarrassed."

"They're going to be more than just embarrassed," he said frankly. "A lot of heads are going to roll because no one took the time to check out your background."

Rosemary looked at her son's tennis shoes under the desk. "My father's friend, Abu Bakr, once told me I was destined for great things, but I wonder what he would say if he saw me now?"

"I'll say one thing. If I wrote a book about you, it would be a best seller."

"What would be your title?"

"Only God Can Judge," he said with certainty. "No one has the right to judge another person, and especially someone like our son!"

"I thought teaching him to read the Quran would help him to

change, but I realized how much I needed changing because of the life I am living!" she said putting on her son's left shoe.

"So, you want me to tell Thomas to convince Phillip Cross about being alive, instead of David?"

"And find out if he remembers scratching David's face after he was shot," she said putting on the other shoe, "and tell him I said happy birthday."

"That's right, it is his birthday and yours too," he said cheerfully. "Happy Birthday, Fatima."

"Thank you," she said tying the laces on both shoes.

Rosemary quickly lost consciousness and fell forward with her forehead propped on top of the desk once again. The Sergeant waited momentarily before helping her to regain consciousness.

"Thomas. . ." he said shaking her by the shoulders.

Rosemary opened her eyes. "Dad, what happened?" she said sitting up straight. "Where is David Cross?"

"David left," he said sitting on the edge of the desk. "I've got a lot to tell you about why you've been reincarnated. Your mother told me everything."

"Really, you talked to my mother?"

"Yes, and she said to tell you Happy Birthday."

SEVENTEEN

"SUPPOSE KING AZAD still wants to marry you and won't release your family until you do?" said Mustafa looking at the City of Antioch off in the distance Fatima and Mustafa rode side by side on their camels and clothed in white garments. "He won't want to marry me now, because I am not fourteen anymore and will be twenty-one soon," she stated.

"No, you are not fourteen anymore, but if he saw the way you danced with a pole, he would wish he was fourteen again."

They both laughed.

"Do you really think he will keep them prisoners if I do not marry him?"

"I do not know, little cousin. However, I would pretend to be dead or sick from some disease, just so that I would not have to marry him."

The thought of her parents remaining in a prison camp never crossed Fatima's mind until now. Mustafa could be right. The king might have someone follow the mother and daughter in hopes of apprehending the daughter. Fatima knew she needed a plan to avoid being captured herself. Pretending to be dead was not a bad idea, but it would be hard because of her popularity in Ta'if as a dancer. Too bad she could not leave the country with her mother and father and go to America, she thought. Maybe Mustafa's sister would help her depart for the United States with her family, so they could live in a place where people are not punished for changing their mind. Fatima looked at the City of Antioch just one mile away and hoping to find an answer very quickly.

EIGHTEEN

ANTIOCH is the third largest city in Syria, with a population of 37,000 citizens, and sits on the east coast of the Mediterranean Sea. The Apostle Paul spent time in the city named after King Antiochus, preaching about Jesus Christ in the Jewish Synagogue and calling those who followed his doctrine, "Christians." Because of Paul's conversion from Judaism to Christianity, a national holiday was declared in Antioch as a tribute to him for adopting a different faith. The Jewish synagogue where Paul began teaching that Jesus Christ was the "Son of God," was not only converted into a Christian Church, but it also became a world-wide tourist site for visitors from all around the globe. Antioch also became the central marketplace to buy and sell food products, livestock, and household goods from the Arab and Jewish merchants during this international celebration.

At age 34, Miriam Akbar was a successful businesswoman, who increased her wealth by importing and exporting products with other countries while living in Antioch. She was also good friends with King Lahore Ibn Azad, having done business with him in the past, and gave Fatima the reward money for finding her long-lost brother and enough dirhams to pay for her parents' release from the prison camp and safe passage back to her estate in Antioch. She also assured Fatima that The King of Saudi Arabia would not trouble her anymore about matrimony again. Fatima was immensely grateful.

Miriam was overjoyed at seeing her brother for the first time in 22 years and quickly offered him the position of being an overseer to the property she owned, which of course he readily accepted because of his experience as a traveling salesman like his father, Ali.

Two days before Fatima's twenty first birthday, Omar and Aisha came face to face with their daughter after being separated for 7 years! Miriam, Mustafa, and Fatima were standing on the property of the estate when Fatima noticed three camels heading in their direction and realized it was her parents coming from the prison camp with all their belongings and ran towards them as fast as she could. Miriam and Mustafa walked towards the new visitors with a smile.

Omar Muttalib's garments were shabby. He appeared to be much older than he was, due to the loss of weight. Aisha also looked thinner and was dressed in rags. Omar dismounted, took off his kufi cap, and smiled as he watched his daughter run towards him. Aisha remained seated on her camel with a look of happiness. Omar took notice of Fatima's clothes. The long dress she wore displayed every line and curve of her shapely figure. She did not think of herself as a little girl anymore, he thought. And something about her choice of clothing made him wonder what kind of life she led in Ta'if. Fatima rushed into her father's arms with tears in her eyes. Omar wiped the tears from her cheeks.

"You look well," he said nodding with approval. Fatima smiled. "You must tell me everything you have been doing," he said holding her by the shoulders.

Mustafa and Miriam walked up to Omar. "As salaamu alaikum, Uncle Omar," said Mustafa with his right hand extended. Mustafa wore black trousers, long white shirt that overlapped his pants, and moccasins made from animal skin. His hair was cut short and trimmed around his head.

"Wa alaikum as salaam," said Omar shaking hands with his nephew and then kissing his cheek. "My brother would be pleased that you and your sister are together again like she always wanted."

Mustafa looked at Miriam. She wore a full-length hijab made of cotton and leather sandals. "My sister was the one who gave King Azad the money in exchange for your freedom as a reward to Fatima for bringing me to Antioch."

"Thank you, Miriam, for paying King Azad the money," he said happily. "I am also happy I was able to put on my brother's sandals and found out how he was murdered."

"So was I," said Miriam gratefully. "And please remember that my home is your home."

Miriam noticed Aisha's complexion as she sat on the camel dressed in rags. Prison camps had a way of aging people no matter who they were, she thought. "How are you doing, Aisha?" said Miriam, with a voice full of joy.

I am doing well and thank you for helping us to see our daughter again," replied Aisha.

Mustafa glanced back and forth at Omar and his sister as he spoke. "What did you mean you put on my father's sandals to find out how he was murdered?" he inquired.

"Your father was able to come back to life because of something known as a Rue, but it's a long story. Perhaps I will tell you how it works one day."

"Fatima, help your mother off the camel," instructed Miriam. "And Mustafa, see that the animals are taken care of."

Fatima made the animal kneel, so her mother could dismount. Aisha wrapped her arms around Fatima. "My daughter is all grown up," she said with watery eyes.

"No, Mother, I am still your little girl," said Fatima bashfully.

Aisha and her daughter strolled arm in arm to the house. Mustafa took the camels by the reins to the corral filled with other livestock being watered and fed.

NINETEEN

THE BEAUTIFUL AND WEALTHY Miriam Akbar resided in a two-story mansion made with clay-bearing soil and filled with furniture crafted from fine wood. Marbled floors were polished with wax. Metamorphic rocks were used to make pillars throughout the residence. The 2nd floor consisted of 12 exquisite rooms for her guests, and a 3rd compartment at the end of the hall where Miriam slept. The hallway was decorated on both sides of the wall with paintings from around the world. The 10 acres owned by the rich heiress was estimated to be worth more than 3 million dirhams. Miriam also had 8-male and 7-female servants living on the property.

The family was met at the door by one of Miriam's African servants. He was 6 feet tall, draped in a black suit, and reminded Omar of an English Butler. Miriam spoke to the African in Arabic, after which he escorted Omar and Aisha to their rooms. Miriam and Fatima went into the dining hall. The hall contained 3 chandeliers hanging from the ceiling and lit with candles. There was a table under the chandeliers with 13 chairs, 6 on each side, and Miriam's chair at the end of the table facing the dining room door. Miriam sat at the head of the table. Fatima was seated on her right side.

"Your mother and father went through quite a bit," said Miriam sadly.

"Yes, I know," agreed Fatima, "and I owe you a lot for what you did."

"You owe me nothing. I never thought I would ever see my brother again and you helped me find the only family I have, so I am indebted to you."

"May I ask you a question?" said Fatima, remembering Miriam was once a dancer in Ta'if.

"By all means."

"Did you tell your husband what you did before you married him because I was wondering if I should tell my father I was a prostitute?"

Miriam leaned forward and folded her hands together like a schoolteacher. "Before I answer that, let me ask you a question. How do you think your father would feel if he found out from someone else?"

"He would be very hurt."

"Then you have answered your own question," she said leaning back against the chair.

"So, you told your husband what you did before you were married?"

"He already knew. You and I are much alike Fatima, because we make our own luck. Whoever you marry better be smart enough not to think of you as just a housewife or you are going to do whatever it takes to prove he's wrong."

Miriam and Fatima were interrupted by Mustafa's voice as he strolled into the dining hall. "What have you two ladies been talking about all alone together?" he said, closing the door behind him.

"Nothing you would be interested in hearing," replied Miriam crossing her legs.

"My dear sister, anything you have to say is always worth listening to," he remarked sitting beside Fatima.

The African servant entered the dining hall and spoke to Miriam.

Miriam nodded her head. "Dinner is ready," she said as the servant walked away. "Fatima, why don't you let your mother and father know it is time to eat."

Before Fatima could leave the table, her parents stepped into the hall and sat at the table on the left side of Miriam. Omar possessed a clean-shaven face and was smartly dressed in silk garments. Aisha was attired in clothes made of satin. "You look beautiful, Mother," said Fatima approvingly.

"Yes, she does," stated Omar happily, "and I have you to thank once again for all you have done, Miriam Akbar."

"Nonsense," responded Miriam waving her hand. "It is my pleasure to reward the Muttalib Family for what all of you have given me. Your brother, Ali, taught Mustafa to be a fine merchant. Fatima has united me with the only relative I ever had. And most of all, we are one family again."

Two female servants walked into the hall carrying food on silver trays and began placing dinner plates on the table in front of everyone. Miriam looked at Omar. "This Saturday will be Fatima's birthday, and I intend to hold a banquet in her honor," she said spreading a napkin across her lap. "I was wondering if you and Aisha would care to go to the marketplace tomorrow with Fatima and Mustafa to buy something to wear for the occasion?"

Omar wrapped one arm around Aisha's shoulder and looked at Fatima as he spoke. "It seems like only yesterday when my daughter would ride on the back of my camel and ask me a thousand questions about life," he said reminiscing. "And now she is old enough to have her own children and I hope they ask her as many questions, so she will know what it feels like."

Everyone laughed, including Fatima.

Omar removed his arm from around Aisha's shoulder and sat up straight. "I think I will go with Fatima and Mustafa to buy something to wear for the party," he began. "I have been to the market many times to sell merchandise and made good money from the tourist who came here to see where the Apostle Paul taught Christianity."

"Ali brought me here a few times when I was just a baby and we made quite a profit from the foreigners ourselves," claimed Mustafa.

"Good, it is settled then," said Miriam slicing a piece of lamb with a knife. "All of you will leave tomorrow and be accompanied by four of my best bodyguards."

"But the marketplace is right down the road," said Mustafa, surprised his sister thought an escort was necessary.

"Yes, the marketplace is nearby, but it will be crowded with visitors from everywhere this weekend to celebrate Paul being a Christian," warned Miriam. "And it is well known that Muslims and Jews have a tendency to start trouble with each other whenever there is a crowd around."

"But we are just going to get something to wear, so what trouble could anyone cause us?" inquired Mustafa.

"Maybe you won't have any problems, but I intend to take every precaution. So, do as I say."

Mustafa nodded his head. "As you wish, my dear sister."

TWENTY

"SO, WHEN SHE PUTS ON MY SHOES, this spirit called a *Ruh* comes back to life because I was murdered and didn't die of a natural death?" said Rosemary sitting in the chair with the tennis shoes on.

"Yep," said the Sergeant seated on the edge of the desk.

"And this whole thing won't be over until I can prove David Cross is the one who shot me?"

"Right."

"Why didn't my mother tell me about this before?"

"Maybe she didn't think it would ever happen to her when she came to America, but she has a plan to prove he's guilty."

"What's the plan?"

"To make Phillip believe you aren't dead and have him tell his son what happened at the apartment when David shot you."

"I thought you said no one would believe I'm Thomas because I look like my mother?"

The Sergeant smiled. "I thought about that. Just remember Phillip is going to believe you after he hears what you have to say. When he asks you where Thomas is, just say he's in a witness protection program for his own safety."

"That's not a good idea, Dad. Why would Thomas need protection, when he has no reason to hide?"

"I was thinking about that too," said the Sergeant quickly. "Just tell Phillip you're being protected because his son might try to kill you again. David is going to wonder how his father knows what happened when there was no one else in the apartment, except you, him, and Frederick Steinberg."

"Okay I get that part, but what about my body at the morgue?"

"Your mother thinks the scar on his face came from you scratching him with your fingernails, so I'm going to the morgue to find out for sure," he assured Rosemary. "In the meantime, get Phillip on the phone and say you want to meet him so the both of you can talk."

"How am I going to meet him with these tennis shoes on?" she said pointing to her feet. "Phillip is going to know something is wrong once he looks at my shoes."

The Sergeant rubbed his chin. "Hmm, I didn't think about that," he confessed. "Didn't you say there was a sweatshirt in the box with the rest of your clothes the mortician gave you?"

"Yeah, but so what?"

"Just wear the sweatshirt with your tennis shoes and act like you've been jogging, and he'll never know the difference."

Rosemary frowned. "Everybody in the whole world knows my mother never jogged a day in her life, so that's not going to work," she said frankly.

"Oh yes it will," he said confidently. "It's not what you look like when you're doing what you're doing, Thomas. It's what you're doing when you're doing it, what you look like you're doing!"

Rosemary laughed. "Now I know why you like being a cop. You just say things like you really know what you're talking about."

"I learned it from your grandfather. But all kidding aside, you've got to make Phillip Cross believe you and Frederick had proof people were being blackmailed for money and the reason David wanted you out of the way."

"Don't worry, I'll make him believe I'm alive."

"When you call Phillip, tell him to meet you in the subway station on Fiftieth street and to come alone."

"Why am I meeting him there?"

"To make sure he comes by himself," said the Sergeant walking to the door. "I'll meet you back here after you talk to him."

The Sergeant walked out of the office. Rosemary picked up the receiver and began dialing the number to the Department of Immigration where Phillip Cross worked.

TWENTY ONE

FATIMA SAT BEHIND HER FATHER on a camel with her arms around his waist and her head resting against his shoulder. It was like old times, she told herself. Omar and Fatima wore white clothes to help ward off the heat from the noon day sun. Mustafa and Aisha were also dressed in light-colored garments to shield themselves from the rays of sunlight, which was soon to be well over 110 degrees. The four bodyguards rode horses instead of camels in the event they had to act quickly and protect everyone. They carried bows and arrows over their shoulders, swords around their waist, and daggers strapped to their ankles.

"I want to tell you something Father," said Fatima with her head pressed against his shoulder blade.

"I am listening," he said cheerfully.

Fatima took a deep breath. "I was a prostitute when I lived in Ta'if because I wanted to make money to buy your freedom from King Azad," she began, "I knew it was not the right thing to do, but I did not want you and my mother to be in prison for the rest of your lives because of me."

Omar knew he was as much to blame for breaching the contract with King Azad and his daughter becoming a harlot. "I noticed the clothes you wore when I first saw you and wondered what kind of life you had lived in Ta'if," he said in a voice that showed no signs of anger. "Now that you have told me what you did, I am not surprised."

Omar looked over his shoulder at his daughter. Fatima lifted her head. "Prophet Muhammad, may the peace and blessing of Allah be upon him, said; A dog was going around a well and was about to die of thirst and an Israeli prostitute took off her shoe and gave the dog some water. So, Allah forgave her because of that good deed. I know you have watered many lives while you stayed in Ta'if because I know the kind of daughter I raised. Why should I be ashamed of what you did knowing why you did it?"

Fatima smiled. "I love you, Father," she said resting on his shoulder again.

TWENTY TWO

AS EXPECTED, the marketplace was crowded with tourists. Israeli and Arab venders stood outside their tents waving their products in the air and beckoning visitors to do business with them. Peddlers shouted at sightseers to buy souvenirs displayed on camel skin covering the ground. Miriam's bodyguards were instructed to separate themselves, so each one of them could protect a family member individually and not leave them alone for any reason. Fatima decided to shop by herself and told everyone she would meet them back at the corral where the camels and horses were being kept within a few hours. She wore a scarf over her head, veil across the face, and accompanied by a 6 foot 3-inch guard. She stood browsing through a collection of magazines from the United States on a wooden table and wondering what it would be like to live in a place where women wore clothes other than religious attire and not treated by men like camels and sheep. A young Caucasian gentleman with short red hair was taking pictures of his twin sister who also had red hair. They were wearing short khaki pants, white tee shirts, and mountain boots. The gentleman was backing away from his sister while snapping pictures and accidentally bumped into Fatima, who was facing the other way. Fatima fell forward onto the table and then to the ground. Two legs on the table broke in half. Before the young man could turn around, he was snatched at the neck by the bodyguard in front of the proprietor who sold the magazines. The young man immediately dropped his camera and threw his hands into the air while the guard held a dagger to his throat. The photographer stared at Fatima, realizing she was being protected like a rich celebrity. The guard looked at Fatima to see if she was hurt. Fatima stood up and dusted herself off. The veil that was across her face was now around her neck.

The young man looked at Fatima. She was very beautiful, he thought. "I'm awfully sorry," he said with his hands in the air.

Fatima looked at the handsome American. "That is okay," she said looking at the guard. "You can release him, Raheem, he meant no harm."

The guard unfastened his grip on the young man's throat and returned his dagger to the holster attached to his ankle.

The young girl with red hair rushed towards her brother. "Robert are you all right?" she said nervously.

"Yeah, I'm okay," he replied picking up the camera.

The proprietor started complaining in Arabic about his broken table. The guard kept his hand on his sword while Fatima argued with him concerning the damage.

"Excuse me," shouted Robert. "I'll pay for everything. Just tell me how much the table and the books cost."

Fatima looked at the girl with red hair and freckles on her cheeks. She was as cute as her brother, she thought. "You do not have to pay for anything," said Fatima to Robert. "I will pay for the magazine and the table."

Robert was surprised the attractive celebrity spoke English so perfectly. "No, I insist you let me pay for everything, since it's the least I can do for the trouble I've caused," he said giving the proprietor American money.

"That is too much," stated Fatima removing the veil from around her neck.

The proprietor smiled. "Allahu Akbar," he said happily.

"You're welcome," replied Robert continuing to look at Fatima. "Would you mind if I took a picture of you?" he asked.

"Why would you do that?"

"To show everyone back in America how beautiful the women are in Antioch," he boasted.

"I do not think so," she said blushing.

"Suppose I make a copy and give one to you?" he suggested. "What about that?"

"How will you be able to give me a copy, when I do not live around here?"

"That won't be a problem. I can take your picture and develop it right here."

Fatima admired his persistence. "Very well, but only one picture," she said deciding not to wear the veil.

"I need for you to think about one thing before I take your picture," he said backing away with the camera.

"What is that?"

"Your bodyguard was going to chop me into little pieces before you told him it was just an accident."

Fatima laughed. Robert snapped her picture. "How far away do you live?" he asked, walking towards Fatima.

"I live at Miriam Akbar's estate."

"You mean, Miriam the rich widow?"

"Yes, have you heard of her?"

"Who hasn't?" he said impressed. "Everyone in America has read articles about how rich she is. Would it be all right if I brought the picture to you there?"

"I supposed it would be all right. Perhaps you and your sister would care to have dinner with us this evening?"

Robert glanced at his sister. "We'd love to, wouldn't we Rosy?" he said placing an arm around his sister's shoulder. "This is my sister, Rosemary Shumsky."

"I am pleased to meet you, Miss Shumsky. My name is Fatima Muttalib."

"It's nice to meet you too," said Rosemary. "Are you a princess or something? You speak English very well."

"No, I am just a Muslim living with a wealthy lady."

"Is that Miss or Mrs. Muttalib?" asked Robert.

"I am not married," said Fatima shyly. "Come, Robert and Rosemary, I will introduce you to my family."

TWENTY THREE

ROSEMARY sat on a bench inside the subway station waiting for Phillip Cross. She wore the dingy white tennis shoes and sweatshirt Thomas had on when he was killed. Rosemary decided to wash the blood stains from off the shirt before putting it on. The time was 1:37 p.m. The station was empty, except for two young boys awaiting the Van Courtland Park uptown train to arrive. Rosemary stared at her shoes wondering if this whole idea of convincing Phillip Cross his son was guilty of murder would work. Suppose he demanded to see Thomas Shumsky in person, what then? Or suppose he didn't care, since it was one cop's word against another? And what if he asked questions only his mother could answer? That would make things even more complicated. Nevertheless, David Cross had to be brought to justice, so this spirit referred to as a *Ruh* could be put to rest.

The clamor of a train approaching the fiftieth street station caught Rosemary's attention. The train stopped. The doors opened. The two young boys boarded the train. The train departed. Phillip Cross stood alone on the platform. He was a heavyset man just like his son and weighed 210 pounds. He was also 6 feet tall and 63-years-old. His salt and pepper mustache gave him the appearance of a wealthy stockbroker. He recognized Rosemary and wondered why she was in a jogging suit and tennis shoes, since she wasn't really the athletic type. He walked towards her in a three-piece suit, pocket watch in his vest, and cordovan-colored shoes.

"Hello Rose, long time no see," he smiled.

Rosemary crossed her legs. "Hello, Mr. Cross," she said with her hands folded on top of her knees.

"How come you're being so formal?" he said, wondering why she called him, Mr. Cross, instead of Phillip. "You aren't taping this conversation, are you?"

Phillip was only teasing about their conversation being recorded but something about Rosemary seemed different from the person he had helped become a United States Citizen twenty-five years ago. She had never jogged a day in her life, so why was she sporting a sweat suit in the middle of the afternoon? It didn't make sense.

Rosemary realized Phillip Cross became suspicious after being called Mr. Cross, and knew she had to play her cards right to avoid any more slip ups. "No, Phillip, there's no one listening to this conversation," she assured him. "I called you here because I didn't want anyone to know about this meeting, except David."

Phillip sat down beside Rosemary. "What's going on? You don't look like your old self," he said placing his left palm on top of her hands.

Rosemary stared at Phillip's hand wondering if his mother and Phillip had been more than just friends. "My son is alive," she said looking at him for some indication he didn't believe her.

Phillip Cross took a few seconds to study Rosemary's face before responding. "Well, I'm sure you're happy about that," he said not knowing what else to say. "When did you come by this information?"

"This morning. He said not to tell anyone but you he was alive and would call me later."

Phillip fell back against the seat. "What's the big deal about keeping everything a secret?" he said, crossing his legs. "I would think everyone would be glad to know he's alive, wouldn't you?"

"No, I wouldn't."

"Why not?"

"Because your son might try to kill him again!" she said calmly.

Phillip Cross wanted to laugh, but her expression made him realize she was gravely serious. "You know David would never do such a thing," he said with uncertainty. "What reason would he have, when it was an accident from the start?"

"David shot me because he knew I had proof you were making immigrants pay money to stay in the country," she said agitated. "So, don't give me that crap about it being accidental because it wasn't."

"What?!" Phillip said suddenly. "What do you mean, David shot you?"

"I meant that he shot Thomas," she said forgetting who she looked like. "But what you need to do is ask your son why he told Thomas before he shot him that his mother's name is, Fatima Muttalib, and wanted by the Arab Government for murder."

The clamor of an express train overtook their conversation as it sped past the station heading south. Rosemary waited for the noise to subside and then continued talking. "Your son is going to know my son is alive and told me everything because they were the only ones in the apartment when David shot him and tried to say it was an accident," she concluded.

Rosemary could see from his expression he believed her and decided to add one more persuasive statement to make sure he had no doubts. "You may not think what I'm saying isn't true, but how would I know what actually happened unless I really spoke with Thomas this morning?" she said as if Phillip was being interrogated.

Phillip Cross sat up in his seat, convinced Rosemary might be telling the truth. "Okay, let's assume Thomas is alive. What do you want from me?" he stated, wondering if there was a proposition on the table.

"To make sure David turns himself in," she said without hesitating. "I'll do all I can to see he gets manslaughter, instead of first-degree murder, since he probably didn't mean to shoot me after I showed up. I mean, before my son showed up."

Something was wrong, thought Phillip Cross. He couldn't put his finger on it, but things didn't add up. He had never known Rosemary to referred to herself as Thomas, which immediately caught his attention, and he had never known her to wear a sweat suit and tennis shoes in the middle of the afternoon. And her decision not to reveal where Thomas was hiding didn't seem right either.

Rosemary decided to say one more thing before Phillip could ask any questions. "David claims my son was killed while he stood at the apartment door, but the scar on David's cheek came from Thomas scratching him with his fingernail before he was murdered."

Phillip Cross began surveying the subway station, wondering what he was going to do, as another express train passed the station heading north.

"Let me make it easy for you, Phillip," said Rosemary rising to her feet. "Bring David by my office this afternoon and the four of us will talk about it."

"Four, what four?" he said puzzled.

"My husband will be there because he wants to get to the bottom of this himself."

"What about Thomas? Why won't he be there?" stated Phillip suspiciously.

Rosemary smiled, knowing she had Phillip over a barrel. "I'll tell Thomas to be there too, how's that?"

Phillip Cross wiped the perspiration from the back of his neck with a handkerchief. "What time do you want us to be there?"

"Four o'clock sharp," she said leaving him to ponder on his son's future.

TWENTY FOUR

MY NAME IS THOMAS EMILIO SHUMSKY. I am fifteen years old, five feet six inches tall, and weigh one hundred and fifty-one pounds. I was born on August twelve, nineteen-forty. Me and my mom were born in the same month and on the same day. I didn't know how important that was, until I was murdered and returned from the dead! But that's a different story from the one I want to talk about right now.

I decided to write this diary because I wanted people to know how I felt about being a homosexual. Many people believe that a person doesn't have to be gay if they don't want to be, which will always be the subject of controversy between those who are gay and those who aren't. However, I want to say personally that while growing up, I wanted to be what society said was normal, but I kept having this attraction towards men instead of women and it drove me crazy. After going to junior high school, I tried dating girls, but women can tell right away if a man is masculine or feminine, so that little trick didn't work either.

I want to take a minute and talk about my mom and dad, because they didn't have a clue about what to do with me. The problem was my mom's religious beliefs prevented her from understanding I was born this way and just as normal as everyone else. My dad's moral convictions stopped him from accepting me as I was because in his mind, I was this mentally disturbed child going through an identity crisis. But they will be telling you how they coped with the situation later in the book.

After enrolling in high school, I decided to start lifting weights, just to see all the male students exercising in their biker's shorts. That's where I first saw another Jewish boy named Frederick Steinberg.

Frederick was captain of the weightlifting team at Dartmouth High School for Boys in Manhattan and very good looking. He was one inch taller than I was and had an extremely nice physique. The one thing I disliked about him was that he would chew his fingernails and then spit them on the ground regardless of where he was. I didn't think he would want to be friends with someone like me, because he was known as a lady's man, but one afternoon David Cross and his skinny friend, Billy Blocker, tried to take my money and Frederick came along just in time to stop them. I was getting a drink of water from the fountain right outside the gymnasium and dressed in my usual black suit, black tie, and skull cap. The skull cap is required by the school for everyone to wear and called a "Yarmulke." David and Billy Blocker were dressed in the same type of clothes. They crept up behind me and attempted to take the money I had in my front pocket. I tried to stop them, but Billy held me around my neck while David began searching through my pockets. As soon as I grabbed his hand, he punched me in the stomach. I dropped my books and fell to the floor. Frederick was coming out of the gym and noticed me crying like a baby and them laughing as though they enjoyed knowing I wouldn't fight back. Frederick was also dressed like everyone else and grabbed my arm to lift me off the floor.

"What happened?" he said picking up my books.

A crowd of students gathered around the fountain while David and Billy continued laughing.

"David and Billy tried to take my money," I said wiping away the tears with one hand and holding my stomach with the other.

"Are you okay?" he asked.

"Yeah," I said feeling embarrassed.

"They didn't get the money you had in your pocket, did they?" he said, staring at David.

"No."

"Come on, let's go."

"You can't protect that sissy for the rest of his life, unless you're a sissy too!" David said as me and Frederick walked away.

"Hold these books," Frederick said handing me the books.

David had broad shoulders like a football player, but Frederick was much stronger. Frederick walked back over to where David stood and smacked him so hard his nose bled. Everyone looked in shock and wondering if David was going to fight back, but he just stood there as if he was afraid to say anything else. I kept wishing Billy Blocker would say something smart, so Frederick would slap him too.

"You outta try picking on someone your own size, punk!" Frederick said looking at David.

Billy Blocker pulled David away from me and Frederick and began walking away. Rabbi Jacob, the Principal of Dartmouth, came bursting through the circle of people to see what everyone was looking at.

"HEY, YOU TWO, STOP RIGHT THERE!" yelled Rabbi Jacob looking at David and Billy.

David and Billy turned around. David's nose had stopped bleeding, but his shirt was stained with blood. There was a look of horror on the principal's face as he stared at David. "What in God's name happened to you?" he said with both fists on his hips.

Rabbi Jacob was a short fat middle-aged man with a bald spot at the back of his head and a skull cap on top of the bald spot. He was wearing a white shirt, thin black tie, and black baggy pants. His pot belly overlapped his belt buckle, and I could see his bare stomach peeking through the shirt, which was unbuttoned at the waist and too small for his body.

David pointed at Frederick. "Freddy hit me because I wouldn't give him and his sissy friend my money," he stated without batting an eye.

Rabbi Jacob dropped his hands. "What sissy friend?" he asked glancing at the other students.

"Right there," Billy said pointing at me.

Rabbi Jacob frowned knowing I wasn't brave enough to kill a mosquito, let alone take someone's money.

"I want you to go straight to my office, Mister Steinberg, and wait until I get there," Rabbi Jacob said to Frederick. The Rabbi looked at David. "And you," he stated as if David wasn't completely innocent, "you come with me to the infirmary."

Rabbi Jacob escorted David by the arm through the crowd. "All right everybody the show is over, you can return to your classrooms now," he said loudly.

Frederick walked towards the principal's office. I ran behind Frederick and tapped him on the shoulder.

"Thanks," I said gratefully.

He smiled. "You just let me know if somebody around here gives you any trouble, little brother," he said continuing to walk down the hall.

"My name's Thomas Shumsky," I said offering him a handshake.

Me and Frederick stopped to shake hands. His grip was firm. "My name's Frederick Steinberg, but everybody calls me Freddy," he said releasing my hand.

"What do you think the rabbi is going to do?"

"Hell if I know, but Rabbi Jacob hates me anyway because I grew up on the other side of the tracks."

"What do you mean?"

"I ain't rich like the people here at Dartmouth, because I was born in Harlem."

"Would you like for me to tell him what happened?"

"Naw, that's okay. All he's going to do is threaten to suspend me from the weightlifting team like he always does because he knows I'm the captain and everybody needs me."

"Are you sure?"

Freddy placed his arm around my shoulder like we were old friends. "Don't you worry about me, little brother," he said squeezing me tightly. "You just let me know if somebody tries to mess with you."

Words cannot describe how I felt after Freddy put his arm around me and promised to protect me from people like David Cross and Billy Blocker. He was like a big brother who wasn't afraid to be seen with me in public.

"Would you mind if I went with you to see the rabbi?"

"Sure, why not? Maybe I'll ask him if I could put you on the team as my assistant."

"You mean it?" I said excitedly.

Freddy made the sign of a crucifix with a righthand over his heart. "Cross my heart and hope to die," he said grinning.

I wanted to give Freddy a big hug, but I didn't want to give him the wrong impression about the way I felt. I wanted us to be friends, not lovers.

Rabbi Jacob's office was located at the end of the hall. On one side of the office was a staircase leading up and down the seven-story building.

On the other side of the stairwell was the men's room. "I'm going to the bathroom and take a piss," I said.

"Okay," Freddy said taking his arm from around my shoulder.

I went inside the bathroom. Freddy waited by the Rabbi's office. The bathroom was empty. I went to the last stall and closed the door. The lock was missing several screws, which made it hard to secure the door shut, so I pushed the door with my shoulder and slid the handle into the lock. The toilet was filled with tissue paper, so I pushed the handle down to flush the paper. The water suddenly backed up. I tried to open the door, but the tissue paper began overflowing before I could slide the handle out of the lock. I jumped on top of the pipe connected to the bowl. The water suddenly stopped, but the floor inside the stall was covered with wet soggy paper from out of the toilet. I was about to lean on the door and open the lock when I heard the Rabbi's voice. Since I was standing on the pipe it appeared as if no one else was inside the bathroom.

"I brought you inside the men's room, Mister Steinberg, because I didn't want anyone to hear what I had to say," Rabbi Jacob said.

I decided to remain hidden and listen to their conversation.

"Let's get one thing straight," he began sternly, "You cannot go around punching people like David Cross, even though you think he deserves it. Do you know who Phillip Cross is?"

"Yeah, he's some kinda bigshot that works for the city."

"Not only that, but he also donates money to this school every year. When he finds out you punched his son, he might try to have charges pressed against you. So, you're suspended from the weightlifting team until I can get to the bottom of this."

"David Cross is a fucking bully, Mr. Jacob," Freddy said angrily. "All he does is pick on people like Thomas because his father's a bigshot. I wasn't going to do anything, but he called me and Thomas a sissy, so I made him take back what he said."

That isn't the way to handle situations, Mister Steinberg," warned the Rabbi. "People like Thomas are going to find it difficult living in a society that believes homosexuality is a sin. That's just the way it is."

Freddy kept silent.

"Listen Frederick, I've known you and your father for a long time, but you're just as stubborn as he is," he said sympathetically. "But let me ask you something. Are you and Thomas involved with each other?"

"What do you mean?" Freddy said, sounding offended. "Involved how?"

"You know, having sex together."

"Naw, it's not like that. I just like him that's all."

"I'm only asking because he may feel differently and that could lead to something else."

"How can you know so much about Thomas, when you've never even met him?"

"Because my son is gay, Mister Steinberg, that's how I know so much!" Rabbi Jacob said with authority. "I had to call Phillip Cross because David used to bully my son like he did Thomas. David even tried to make Mathew have sex with him, but Mathew refused and told me about it."

"WHAT A MINUTE, YOU MEAN DAVID CROSS LIKES TO FLIPFLOP TOO?" Freddy said loudly.

"Keep your voice down, Frederick," Rabbi Jacob said quickly. "I'm certainly not going to insinuate that David is bisexual too, because I don't have any proof, but between you and me, this conversation never took place. You get my meaning?"

"Yeah, I got you," Freddy said laughing. "Now I understand why he tried to take the money from Thomas. He really likes him."

"You didn't hear that from me," whispered the Rabbi.

"Well, I'll be damned," Freddy said softly. "Pretending to be a bully was all a fake. And to think he had the nerve to call me a sissy."

"Listen Frederick, I've got to suspend you for a little while to cover my ass, so I need for you to stay out of trouble and keep your nose clean until this whole thing blows over."

"Don't worry, I'm cool," Freddy said as though he understood.

Freddy and the principal left the men's room. I unlocked the door and ran out of the lavatory to find Freddy. He was walking down the staircase. "HEY FREDDY!" I yelled over the banister. "WAIT FOR ME…"

Freddy turned around and remained on the steps until I caught up with him. "Where did you go; I thought you was going to the bathroom?"

"I did, but I had to stand on the water pipe because the toilet broke down after I tried to flush the paper."

Freddy grinned. "That's why he didn't see you when he looked under the doors to make sure no one else was inside."

Freddy started biting his fingernails as we walked downstairs together.

"So, you must have heard what the rabbi said about David trying to bully his son, Mathew?" he said, spitting his nails on the steps.

I stopped at the bottom stairwell and looked at Freddy. "I didn't know Mathew was the Rabbi's son, did you?"

"No, I was a surprised too."

"I heard what he said about David's father pressing charges against you for hitting his son, but I've got an idea."

"What's that?"

"My mom is a superior court judge, and she might be able to stop David's father from doing anything because she knows Mr. Cross personally."

"Well, if you think she can help, it's all right with me," he said looking for more nails to bite.

"Good. Let's go down to the courthouse and I'll talk to her right now."

Me and Freddy took the subway train to the Criminal Court Building on One Hundred Centre Street. I was hoping my mom could help Freddy, just in case Phillip Cross decided to try and have Freddy arrested. The idea of David Cross being bisexual never crossed my mind until I overheard the conversation between Freddy and the Rabbi. I kept wondering if Rabbi Jacob was ashamed of his son being gay. Mathew was a senior at Dartmouth and a very friendly person. Everyone knew he was gay but didn't know he was related to the principal because Mathew's last name was Nowitzki, not Jacob.

TWENTY FIVE

FATIMA INTRODUCED ROBERT AND ROSEMARY SHUMSKY to her family at the corral inside the marketplace. Mustafa was not only pleased she invited the sexy American male and his sister to have dinner that evening, he also insisted they stay as guests until returning to the United States. Robert and his sister accepted the invitation, packed their clothes at the motel where they were staying, and accompanied everyone back to the luxurious 2nd story mansion owned by the rich heiress. The Shumsky Twins received a warm welcome from Miriam upon their arrival. After seeing the snapshot of Fatima at the marketplace, Miriam not only consented to let Robert Shumsky take pictures of her property, but she also suggested he take photographs of the guests being invited to Fatima's birthday celebration on Saturday evening.

Miriam was seated at the head of the dining room table, with Mustafa sitting at the other end facing his sister. As Always, he was decorated in expensive apparel. Miriam wore a silk dress as she admired pictures of her employees feeding animals at the corral in the hot afternoon sun. Omar, Aisha, and Fatima were on the left side of Miriam casually dressed in clothes made of cotton. The Shumsky Twins were seated on the right side of the rich heiress wearing khaki pants and tee-shirts like they were on a safari. The crystal chandeliers above the dining table were lit with candles and gave the entire hall an enjoyable atmosphere for dining.

"These pictures of my employees, and especially the one you took of Fatima, are marvelous, Mr. Shumsky," said Miriam looking at him from the photos. "How long have you been a photographer?"

"I'm not really a photographer, I just do it as a hobby," he replied modestly.

"I think you should consider becoming a professional," she said giving Omar the photographs. "Have you seen this picture of Fatima, it is really gorgeous?"

Omar browsed through the snapshots. "These are excellent, Mr. Shumsky," he agreed. "How old are you if you do not mind me asking?"

"I'm twenty-three, sir,"

"Why don't you want to be a professional?" he asked leaning back against the chair."

"Because my sister and I come from a family of policemen, and that's what we're going to be."

"A policeman, both of you intends to become policemen?" said Omar surprised.

"I planned to become one, but my sister may have trouble, because the department doesn't allow females to become policemen. My grandfather believes it's discrimination not to allow someone to become an officer because they are not of a certain height, or are females, and is fighting a Federal Law that prevents them from being a cop. If he wins, Rosemary could be the first female officer in New York City."

Robert put his arm around his sister's shoulder.

"That is if she can pass the physical," he said squeezing her tightly.

"That would certainly be quite an accomplishment for women," said Miriam folding her hands together. "I wish you much success, Miss Shumsky."

"Thank you," said Rosemary gratefully, "but I told my grandfather that if I don't become a cop, I can still fight those laws that discriminate against us because I only have one more year left before I take the bar examination and become a lawyer."

"How old are you, Miss Shumsky?" inquired Omar.

"I'm twenty-three too."

"Your grandfather sounds like a very smart man, and I am sure you will make him proud whether you become a policeman or not," said Omar giving the pictures to Fatima.

"Well, I really hope she does become a cop, because she's his favorite child," stated Robert kissing her cheek.

Rosemary playfully slapped her brother on the arm. "Don't say that, Bobby," she said embarrassed. "Grandpa doesn't like me more than he does you."

"Oh yes he does and don't try to pretend he doesn't. If something happens to you, he will go crazy. And so would my father."

Rosemary leaned back against the chair, knowing her brother spoke the truth. It was obvious to everyone that Robert and his sister were fond of each other. Fatima looked at the twins wishing she had a big brother like Robert Shumsky.

"Excuse me, Mr. Shumsky, but may I ask you a personal question?" said Mustafa grinning like a news reporter.

"Sure, go ahead."

"Do you really want to be a policeman or are you doing it to please your family?" he said curiously. "I am only asking because you certainly have an eye for beauty and this hobby of yours seems to be what you really enjoy doing."

The handsome American appeared to be at a loss for words, thought Mustafa.

"I think being a policeman is more important than taking pictures, even if he does want to be a photographer," said Fatima putting the stack of snapshots on the table in front of her.

Everyone was surprised Fatima defended Robert before he could speak up for himself. Omar pulled his chair closer to the table, expecting to see a cat fight between his daughter and Mustafa, especially since she enjoyed debating when she thought she was right.

"I wish there were more people like Robert," she continued, "because he puts family tradition above something he may like to do personally."

"Thank you, Miss Muttalib," said Robert smiling. "It's nice to know you understand what family tradition means."

"Why don't you call me Fatima, Robert," she said as if the honor was hers.

"Well, my dear brother, what do you have to say now?" said Miriam smartly. "It seems like Fatima makes a good point."

Mustafa sat up in his chair as if he wasn't defeated just yet. "It's interesting they both consider family tradition to be important, because she has a hobby that could become a tradition like the one he has," he said cleverly.

"What hobby is that?" asked Miriam.

"Belly dancing! She is well known throughout the Town of Ta'if as one of the sexiest performers anyone has ever seen, and I took the liberty of inviting a group of women she has danced with to be here for the party."

Everyone looked at Fatima. Fatima stared at Mustafa as though she had been betrayed. Aisha began tugging on the sleeve of her daughter's dress. "You were a belly dancer, Amina?" she said alarmed.

"Yes Mother, I used to dance," she sighed. "It is a long story as to why I started, but I do not dance anymore."

"But you will honor us with a performance when the other girls arrive won't you, Sarah?" teased Mustafa.

"Oh yes, Miss Muttalib, please do," Rosemary urged. "My brother and I would love to see you and the other women dance. Wouldn't we Bobby?"

There was a knock at the dining room door, after which the African servant entered the hall and walked over to Miriam. He bent forward and whispered into her ear. Miriam gave the servant a nod. The African returned to the door and opened it, so the visitors could enter. Fourteen beautiful women strolled into the hall and began admiring the chandeliers and marbled floor like tourists in a museum. They wore colorful hijabs to go along with their glamorous hairstyles. Abu Bakr strutted into the dining room like a Sultan Sheik. He was draped in clothing made of silk and satin and looked around at the majestic architecture of Miriam Akbar's establishment with admiration.

One of the women was on crutches and quickly noticed Fatima. "Sarah!" she said elated.

Fatima rose from her chair and smiled. The other dancers rushed to gather around Fatima and showered her with kisses on the cheek. "Where have you been, Sarah?" said Sasha with crutches under her arms. "You promised to come back, but it has been over three months."

"Abu Bakr brought us here and said we were going to dance with you again. Is that true?" said the dancer with an albino complexion.

"Yes, it's true," said Fatima.

"This place is beautiful, Sarah," said the brunet staring at the chandeliers above her head. "No wonder you did not want to come back to Ta'if right away."

"Ladies, ladies, where are your manners?" said Abu Bakr clapping his hands together. "Let us not forget we are guests of Mustafa and his charming sister, Miriam Akbar."

Sasha turned around on her crutches to face the rich widow. "Abu Bakr said you used to live in Ta'if before you became rich and famous," she said with envy.

Miriam rose from the table and walked towards the ensemble. "Abu Bakr speaks the truth," she said standing in front of Sasha. "And I owe him a great deal for watching over me when I stayed in his boarding house just like all of you do"

"My name is Sasha, Your Grace," she said bowing her head.

"I am not a queen, Sasha. Just a plain old-fashioned widow with money. And who are these other beautiful ladies?"

"We are the Ta'if Dancers and Sarah dances with us too!" boasted the albino.

"Who is Sarah?"

"Right there. . ." said the brunet pointing at Fatima.

Miriam laughed. "Well, Sarah, would you please show our guests to their rooms while I chat with Abu Bakr?"

Fatima escorted the ensemble to the second floor. Abu Bakr walked over to Miriam and held her by the shoulders. "It was very gracious of you to pay for Omar and Aisha's freedom," he said approvingly. "Your fame and fortune has spread far and wide because of your generosity. May Allah continue to bless you my child with even more than you have already."

"Thank you."

Abu Bakr strolled towards Omar with open arms. Everyone watched them hug one another other like old friends. "Thank you for taking care of my daughter," said Omar, his eyes swelling with tears.

"Actually, she took care of me and many of the people she danced with," replied Abu Bakr. "Your daughter is destined to become someone of great character because of her charming personality."

"That is true," agreed Mustafa, walking towards Abu Bakr and Omar. "I am the one who sent you the invitation for Fatima's celebration."

Abu Bakr and Mustafa shook hands.

"We have never met, but everyone speaks very highly of you," said Mustafa releasing Abu Bakr's hand.

"Really?" said Abu Bakr noticing Mustafa's feminine way of shaking hands. "I hope what you have heard is not true."

Mustafa smiled, while Everyone laughed.

Mustafa turned towards the Shumsky Twins. "This handsome young man and his lovely sister are also our guests," he said cordially. "Robert and Rosemary, this is Abu Bakr."

Robert and Rosemary smiled. "Hello," they said simultaneously.

Abu Bakr bowed his head. "It is my pleasure."

"Well now that everyone has been introduced, I think it is time to eat," said Miriam returning to her seat. "Mustafa, see that more chairs are brought to the table please."

"With pleasure my dear sister," he said walking out of the dining hall.

TWENTY SIX

ME AND FREDDY walked into the courtroom. My mom was wearing a black robe and sitting on the judge's bench. The courtroom was empty. A negro lady wearing a wool dress was sitting at her desk on the left side of the bench talking to my mom. Freddy followed me as I went to the long table in front of the bench where the lawyers stood when speaking to the judge. My mom noticed me and Freddy standing at the table. "What are you doing here, Emilio?" she said smiling.

My mom began calling me Emilio when I was very young. It means to be industrious. The name Thomas just means "Twin", and I think she enjoyed calling me by a name that had more meaning. "This is my friend Frederick Steinberg," I said putting my books on the table. "Freddy, this is my mom."

"It is nice to meet you, Mr. Steinberg."

"Hello, ma'am. I mean, Your Honor," he said putting his hands behind his back like a boy scout.

"Is everything all right?" she asked.

"Can we talk in private mom?" I said before explaining why I brought Freddy to the courthouse.

"Let's go into my chambers."

Me and Freddy followed her into the office. I had been inside my mom's chambers before and was always fascinated by the different types of law books in shelves on the wall and thinking she had to be a very smart to become a judge.

"Why don't both of you have a seat?" she said pointing to the sofa against the wall by the bathroom door.

Me and Freddy sat down. She sat behind a mahogany desk in the middle of the office facing us. There was a photograph on the desk of her and my dad on their wedding day. Every time I saw that photo I wondered if I was born to be gay because I looked exactly like my mother!

"Okay, what is the problem?" she said, folding her arms together.

"Freddy slapped David Cross because he tried to take my money and Rabbi Jacob said David's father is going to press charges when he finds out that Freddy slapped his son. So...,"

"Wait a minute," she said raising her hand like a traffic cop. "You are talking too fast, Emilio. Slow down and do not talk so fast."

I calmly told her what happened at the water fountain in school. Then I told her what Freddy, and the rabbi talked about inside the men's room. I didn't say anything about the rabbi's son being gay for reasons I didn't think it was important. I also didn't mention that David Cross might be bisexual, since no one knew for sure, and I didn't want to start any rumors.

My mom looked at Freddy. "I want to thank you for what you did to help my son, Mr. Steinberg," she said with appreciation. "And I will try to do all I can to prevent Phillip from pressing charges, so you do not have to worry about that."

"Thanks," he said.

I began wondering if my mom and David's father were more than business associates because of the way she called him Phillip. I learned a few years later they were more than just associates, but that's another story.

"Sometimes people can be very cruel, Emilio, but you must learn not to let what they say affect you," she said sounding like Rabbi Jacob.

Freddy began chewing on his thumb nail. "Can I say something, Your Honor, if you don't mind?" he asked before spitting the nail on the floor.

"Yes, Mr. Steinberg, go right ahead."

"If people think they can bully you they'll do it every time," he began. "Thomas needs to learn how to fight so he can protect himself, because I can't be around all the time to help him."

"And what kind of fighting do you think he needs to learn, Mr. Steinberg?"

"Karate!" he said grinning. "I know a place where they teach you all kinds of judo and he can learn right away."

My mom looked at me again. "So now you want to go to karate school?"

I wondered if she thought me and Freddy had this all planned out before coming to the courthouse. "Yes," I nodded up and down.

"How much will it cost, Mr. Steinberg?"

"About two hundred bucks."

"And you are sure this is what you want to do?" she said once more.

"Yep," I said eagerly.

My mom walked to the clothes rack by the door and took her purse off the hook on the rack. She took an American Express Card from out of her wallet and gave it to me. "Use this to pay for the karate class," she said as if she was glad, I wanted to protect myself, "and then you and Frederick go to a restaurant because I won't be home until late and there is nothing at the house to eat."

TWENTY SEVEN

THE KARATE SCHOOL was in a two-story building at the corner of ninety sixth street and Broadway and called, "The Art of Self Defense." On the second floor were three large studio rooms filled with young people of all nationalities wearing white karate suits and practicing martial arts with each other. Two young Japanese girls came out of the room near the entrance without shoes and wearing karate clothes.

"How much does it cost to sign up for a karate class?" Freddy asked.

"Are you a student in school somewhere?" the thin Japanese girl with brown hair said.

"Yeah, we go to Dartmouth High, so do we get a discount?"

The other female was heavyset and had black hair. "Yes, but you must fill out an application and pay fifty dollars for six months," she said with an accent.

"We want to pay for two years and be a black-belt when we're finished," Freddy said sounding self-assured.

Both girls giggled. "Come with us," the thin girl said.

Me and Freddy were escorted to an office on the same floor. I began thinking that if these two females were learning how to fight, I certainly had nothing to be ashamed of. A very attractive Caucasian female of about seventeen, sat behind a desk wearing gold framed eyeglasses and a grey sweatshirt with Dartmouth High School printed on the front. She had dark hair that was parted down the middle and fell to her shoulders. Her breasts were at least a C-cup size. To say she was beautiful would be an understatement. She was gorgeous from head to toe, and she knew it!

"I just want to ask you one question," Freddy said with his hands in his pants pockets and smiling. "Does your boyfriend go to the school on that shirt you're wearing?"

"Are you here to sign up for the self-defense classes?" she said ignoring his question.

"No, my friend is," he said pointing his thumb at me. "I already know how to defend myself."

The two girls walked away. The female behind the desk handed me an application on a clipboard. "Please fill this out and give it back to me when you're finished," she said politely.

I took a seat by the office door and began filling out the questionnaire, while Freddy kept talking to the receptionist. It was obvious she wasn't interested in being friends and a little while later, insisted he stop asking her so many questions. Freddy finally sat down next to me.

"Did you find out where she got the sweatshirt from?" I asked.

"She said it belonged to her brother but wouldn't tell me his name."

"What's her name?"

"Katheryn."

"Katheryn what?"

"She wouldn't tell me that either," he said disgusted.

I finished answering the questions and gave the application back to the receptionist. Freddy stood beside me with his hands behind his back.

"You want to register for two years?" she said surprised.

"Yes," I said giving her the credit card.

"But this says, Rosemary Shumsky?"

"It belongs to my mother," I said folding my arms together like my mom does. "She's a Superior Court Judge and my name is Thomas Shumsky."

"Please wait, while I ask the manager about this?"

The receptionist rose from her chair and walked out the door. The tight pair of dungarees she wore made her look very sexy. A few minutes later, she returned with a sale receipt printed from the credit card. "I'm sorry to keep you waiting, but the manager had to approve it first," she said giving me the card.

I put the card in my coat pocket and signed the receipt. She tore the carbon copy of the slip from the invoice and gave me the receipt, "Your first class will start on Saturday morning at nine o'clock."

"Thanks," I said putting the receipt in my pocket.

"Will you be working this Saturday?" Freddy asked.

The receptionist quickly frowned. "Yes I will," she said looking irritated.

"Good, I'll see you then."

"I thought you said you didn't like karate?"

"I never said I didn't like it, I just said I already know how to defend myself."

The receptionist frowned again and sat down behind the desk. Me and Freddy walked out of the office and down the staircase. Freddy wrapped his arm around my shoulder as we stepped outside the building. The weather was cold.

"That foxy girl upstairs is going to be a hard nut to crack," he said as we walked to the subway station.

"I don't know, Freddy. She acts like she's really not interested in wanting to know you."

Freddy started imitating the Rabbi. "Listen, Frederick, I've known you and your father for a long time and you're just as stubborn as he is."

I started laughing.

Freddy stopped walking and took his arm from around my shoulder. "And that's exactly what it's going to take to get that foxy girl to be friends. Good old-fashioned stubbornness."

We both laughed very loudly.

"What do you want to eat?" I asked.

"How about some sirloin steaks?" he recommended. "I happened to know where the best restaurants are in Harlem. Just follow me my good man and let me take you through a place known all over the world as the ghetto."

Something told me Frederick Steinberg and I were going to be good friends, and words cannot describe how happy it made me feel.

TWENTY EIGHT

SERGEANT ROBERT BERNARD SHUMSKY had visited the morgue more times than he cared to remember and could never get over feeling nauseous when viewing dead bodies being cut open as if they were in a butcher shop. This was the second time he had come to identify his son's corpse. The first time he witnessed Thomas laying lifeless on the table things didn't seem right. The bullet went straight through his body as though he had been shot at close range. However, the report written by Detective David Cross said Officer Thomas was shot accidentally while standing at his apartment door fifteen feet away from where the gun was. But how could a bullet shell hit someone fifteen feet away make the same type of wound when shot at close range? Sergeant Shumsky knew it was impossible but decided not to try and prove it was true, even though the mortician agreed with his theory. And the fact of the matter was, close range or not, Thomas was dead and that was that.

Now Robert Bernard Shumsky was here at the morgue for the second time and things were different. Officer Thomas was shot at close range just as he suspected. And, more importantly, Thomas was alive! What the Sergeant needed was a concrete evidence that his son wasn't shot fifteen feet away. Hopefully, there would be fragments of skin cells under Tommy's fingernails from the face of David Cross to prove Thomas wasn't at the door.

"I've been examining bodies for fifty-three years and have never seen a corpse like this before," said James Miller, while scraping particles from under Thomas Shumsky's fingernails with a scalpel.

"What do you mean, Jimmy?" said the Sergeant standing beside his son's body.

James Miller was dressed in a white laboratory jacket. He was

73 years old and one of the first Negro morticians to have his own business. The grey mustache and horn-rimmed spectacles on the tip of his nose gave him the look of an old-fashioned undertaker. "Rigor mortis usually sets in when a person has been dead for more than twelve hours, but this corpse is different," he said taking off his glasses. "It's almost as if he wasn't dead."

The Sergeant grinned, knowing he understood something about his son the mortician didn't.

"I'll tell you something else," James Miller went on to say, "the blood that was on your son's sweatshirt belongs to the other guy that was killed."

"You mean, Frederick Steinberg?"

"Yes."

The Sergeant made a mental note to remind himself to ask Thomas about Frederick's blood on his sweatshirt. "Is there enough skin in that dish to prove it came from David's face?" he asked.

"I'll have to look at it through a microscope, but if I was a gambling man I wouldn't be afraid to put up some money."

The Sergeant glanced at his wristwatch. It was 1:45 p.m. He wondered if Thomas was talking to Phillip Cross at the fiftieth street subway station "How long would it take you to look at with a microscope, Mr. Miller?"

"About ten minutes."

"Let's do it."

James Miller took the dish with skin cells into the laboratory. The room was full of medicine cabinets with glass doors on the walls. There was a desk in the corner of the compartment beneath the cabinets. On top of the desk rested a gigantic microscope. The mortician put the specimen under the optical instrument and adjusted the lens to get a closer look at the skin fragments. After examining the specimen, he returned to the room where the Sergeant continued standing beside the body.

"Yep, it's someone's skin all right," he said shaking his head.

"And I'll tell you something else. It belongs to a white man too."

"Are you sure?" the Sergeant asked as he pushed the front end of his hat upwards with one finger.

"I've been doing this for fifty-three years, Robert, and I ought to know a white man's skin from my own!"

"Listen Jimmy, I need for you to hide my son's body just in case someone wants to see if he's really dead."

"What do you mean hide him, hide him where?"

"I don't know. Any place you can find right now."

"Listen Robert, I could get into trouble if I don't write out an autopsy report about the people I examine. It's the law."

"Can you hide his body for just a few hours more?" begged the Sergeant. "I'll explain everything to you later, but right now I need you to stall anybody that ask any questions about my son. Will you do that for me?"

"I'll give you twenty-four hours. That's the best I can do."

"Thanks, Jimmy, I owe you one," said the Sergeant adjusting his hat and walking out the door.

Robert Shumsky decided not to take the report written by James Miller about Frederick Steinberg's blood being on his son's shirt, because he wasn't sure if he needed more proof than he already had. However, he did know there was enough evidence to show the skin of David's face was under Tommy's fingernails.

TWENTY NINE

IT WAS 7:00 IN THE EVENING. The desert sun was now behind the hills of Antioch. There was a warm and mild temperature throughout the city. Miriam Akbar's dining hall was converted into a theater. There was an 8-foot pole made from a bamboo tree secured to the floor at center stage and looked exactly like the pole made in Ta'if. The dignitaries, aristocrats, and those of royalty were waiting to see the Ta'if Dancers perform in honor of Fatima's Birthday Celebration. Additional employees were used to serving all kinds of exotic food and beverages to the 150 guests. Miriam stood up from the chair with a silver goblet in her hand. She was dressed in a white silk gown trimmed with gold and satin slippers laced with emeralds. On her head was a hat with diamonds like those worn by the Catholic Pope. She looked like the Good Witch from the West in the movie, "Wizard of Oz!"

"Ladies and gentlemen, may I have your attention please," said Miriam tapping her goblet with a silver spoon.

Everyone looked at the hostess.

"Today is Fatima Muttalib's twenty first birthday. You are going to see someone with extraordinary courage perform in front of you as a dancer. Fatima's father agreed to let her marry King Lahore Ibn Azad. But after talking to Fatima, he decided not to honor the agreement with King Azad, because he realized that Fatima should be the one to decide who she marries. Fatima's parents were thrown into a prison camp for refusing to let their only child marry the king. Fatima then went into hiding at the Town of Ta'if because her father wanted to make sure his daughter's whereabouts would remain unknown. While living in Ta'if, Fatima taught herself how to dance, so she could try and make enough money to buy back her parent's freedom from the king."

Miriam looked at Omar and Aisha. They were dressed like the King and Queen of England.

"Fatima's mother and father are here tonight," Miriam went on to say, "because of their daughter's determination to do whatever it took to liberate her family from King Azad's prison camp. Now her parents are free to be with you and I this evening to pay tribute to their daughter as she performs with a renowned group known as the Ta'if Dancers."

Miriam raised her goblet in the air.

"Please stand up and give a toast to Fatima's mother and Father. Mr. and Mrs. Omar Muttalib," she said ceremoniously.

Everyone stood on their feet and drank from silver goblets to commemorate Fatima's parents. Omar and Aisha also stood up from their chairs and smiled.

"And now, without further ado. Here they are, Fatima and the Ta'if Dancers," said Miriam waving her arm towards the stage.

Candle lights on two of the chandeliers hanging from the ceiling were extinguished by Abu Bakr, who used a long stick to put out the flames. The dining hall looked like the inside of a night club. Three voluptuous belly dancers emerged from behind the curtain carrying instruments. They wore baggy trousers made from silk cloth, veils across their faces, and red brassieres. Every other part of their body was exposed. Attached to their navels were earrings made of gold. On their feet were red slippers with the toes curled up like the front end of an Aladdin's lamp. The trio sat on the floor with their legs crossed in front of the audience. The first instrumentalist strummed a small harp made with seven strings. The second musician played a flute. The third member used a drumstick to bang on a tom-tom between her legs. The music was played in a slow rhythm with the serene melody of a snake charmer.

The curtain opened. Ten more dancers were seated on the floor around the 8-foot pole facing the audience and dressed identically like the musicians. The dancers were without slippers and had red enamel polish on their toenails. Each dancer used a tambourine to bang against their hands in rhythm to the music. Fatima Muttalib was standing at the pole without shoes and blind folded. Her hands were tied to the pole as if she was being burned at the stake. She wore a fishnet nightgown and bright red panties under the gown. The cosmetics on her face made her look as white as snow. The women with tambourines stood on their feet and yelped like Indians while dancing around the pole in perfect step to the tom-tom. The audience was completely captivated by what they were seeing. The music came to a halt. The dancers circled the pole. Two women untied Fatima's hands and removed the blindfold. Fatima turned around and scaled the pole towards a rope extending at the top. She grabbed the rope. The musicians started playing a very fast rhythm. Fatima twirled like a top as she held the rope with one hand. The dancers slapped the tambourines against their hips and strutted around the tables and throughout the dining hall. Fatima wrapped her legs around the pole, released the rope, and slid head first down to the bottom with her hands out stretched like a bird.

All the guests jumped to their feet and cheered with excitement after witnessing Fatima come to a sudden stop at the very bottom with just the use of her legs. Everyone remained standing and clapped to the music as she bedazzled them with acrobatic twists and turns around the pole. Every movement of her shapely anatomy was a sight to behold. The dancers returned to the stage and demonstrated their own skillful agility with the pole one by one.

THIRTY

FATIMA AND HER SUPPORTING CAST were showered with applause after their performance. Never had anyone seen a group of women display such sensuous techniques with a pole. Especially Fatima Muttalib. She wasn't just a dancer: she was a hypnotist that could induce a spell over an entire audience with effortless grace. Robert Shumsky never imagined the beautiful and intelligent girl he met at the marketplace would be a belly dancer. To say he was dumbfounded would be an understatement. He was flabbergasted beyond words and took pictures of every acrobatic move she made from the time she scaled the pole until she landed at the bottom. He knew those photographs were worth a lot of money once he sold them to the right magazine company. No one in the United States had ever danced like these Arab women, he told himself. Too bad he couldn't persuade them to come to America. They would be the envy of every dance group in the world after they became internationally known. Wait a minute, why couldn't he convince them to come to the United States, he wondered. All they needed was a passport. Phillip Cross could get them one in no time since he worked for the Department of Immigration. The more Robert Shumsky thought about it, the more he believed Fatima and the Ta'if Dancers would relish the idea of becoming rich and famous chorus girls. Particularly Fatima, whose life was somewhat the same as Miriam Akbar. The only difference was Miriam happened to stumble upon a rich man who left her his estate after he died. Whereas Fatima was her own meal ticket. She had beauty, charm, and talent all rolled into one.

"YES-SIR-RE-BOB," said Robert Shumsky to himself. "THE TA'IF DANCERS WERE ABOUT TO BECOME THE GREATEST SHOW ON EARTH!" All he had to do was choose the right time and place to disclose a very simple business plan. He took pictures while Fatima and the Ta'if Dancers performed in a theater filled with people. Very simple.

Hold on a second, thought Robert, realizing he had another bright idea. Why not ask Fatima to accompany him and his sister tomorrow morning to the well-known synagogue where the famous Apostle Paul once taught Christianity? Once they were alone, it would be the perfect time to spring his idea on the beautiful and talented dancer. As soon as she agreed to come to America the others were sure to follow. He might even be lucky enough to make Fatima his girlfriend and win all the way around. But that was a long way off and right now the objective was to get her to America, not to a bedroom suite in a hotel room.

THIRTY ONE

THE TIME WAS 2:14 P.M. Rosemary was back inside the judge's chambers feeling like she had won the first round of a boxing match at the subway station with Phillip Cross. However, she also knew the fight was far from over. Phillip Cross wasn't about to let his son go to prison while he just stood by and did nothing. And David Cross made it clear in the apartment after shooting Frederick Steinberg that he knew about his mother and father being wanted by the Arab Government for murder and threatening to tell the authorities in the United States, so he wouldn't have to go to prison. Nevertheless, everything was going as planned. Phillip Cross was undoubtedly worried about his son's future. And that was a good thing for starters, thought Rosemary as she took off the sweat suit, placed it back inside the box on the couch, and put on the black robe again. There was a knock at the door. "Come in," she said.

The Sergeant strolled into the chambers looking bright and cheerful. "I have some great news," he said closing the door and grinning like a Halloween Pumpkin. "The mortician said the skin under your fingernails belong to a Caucasian, but he still needs samples from David Cross to prove it came from his face."

Rosemary took a seat on the couch. "That's great, Dad," she said glumly.

"What's the matter?"

"Phillip Cross acted really chummy with me before I told him why I wanted to talk, and I got the feeling that him and my mother were more than just friends."

"They were more than just friends, but I have to blame myself for letting that happen," he said knowing his wife's infidelity was old news.

"You mean you knew about them being involved and never said anything?"

The Sergeant took a moment to study Rosemary's face. "Marriage can be complicated sometimes, Tommy," he sighed. "I've known a lot of things about your mother and never said anything. We still care about each other and want to work things out, but it won't be easy because we were never in love to begin with."

"Why did you get married?"

"We thought it was the right thing to do at the time. She needed a new identity, and I wanted to repay her for saving my life, so we got hitched up."

The Sergeant took a seat on the couch alongside Rosemary and placed his hat beside the box. "Sometimes I think cops shouldn't get married at all," he said sorrowfully. "Even though my mother understood what being married to my father would be like, she was never the same after he broke his promise and was killed."

"What promise?"

"He promised to get a desk job after he was shot by a drug dealer and nearly died. After I told him how my sister was murdered by the Arab Soldiers in Antioch, he became depressed because he really wanted her to be a cop and went back to be a detective again. That's when he and mother starter arguing about the promise he made to get a desk job."

"And that's when he got killed during that drug raid in the Greenwich Village?" said Rosemary finishing the story.

"And he told me to tell her not to be angry before he died. Then she asked me to get a desk job because I was all she had left."

"So, what are you going to do, be a desk sergeant until you retire?" she said hoping he had an answer to his dilemma.

The Sergeant leaned back and placed his arms over the backseat. "Sometimes I think that wouldn't be a bad idea," he said frowning. "My father's dead, my sister was killed in Antioch, and her grandson's been murdered. I know she would die of a broken heart if something happened to me."

"Why don't you have some more children?" suggested Rosemary. "It's not too late and might help you and mom to start over."

"Your mother and I are way passed having any more children, Tommy. She's forty-nine and I'm fifty-one, just in case you didn't know it."

"Age is just a number, Dad," she said with arms folded. "You claimed you got married for the wrong reasons, maybe it's time you did something for the right reasons."

The thought of raising more children wasn't what Robert Shumsky had in mind, but on the other hand it wasn't a bad idea either.

"And I want you to do me a favor if you do have some more kids."

"What's that?"

"Find someone like me, so you can give him some of the things I never got!"

"Your mother and I gave you everything you could have possibly needed, Thomas," he announced quickly, "and I think you're being a little unfair when you say that."

"You gave me everything except the feeling that I didn't need to change myself."

"Yeah, I know, and that's the main reason why I will never treat anyone else the way I did you."

"Good," she smiled. "Now let's talk about what we're going to do when Phillip and David show up this afternoon."

THIRTY TWO

FREDDY TOOK ME TO A JAPANESE RESTAURANT, located on one hundred and twenty fifth street, between Amsterdam and Convent Avenue, in upper Manhattan. It was a small establishment with an occupancy of one hundred customers and nicely decorated with oriental furniture and pictures on the wall of people living in Tokyo, which is the Capital of Japan. I used to wonder what the difference was between the Japanese and Chinese people and found out it was just the types of food they ate.

Across the street from the restaurant were three buildings, twenty-one stories high, called the GRANT PROJECTS. Majority of the residents were Negros and Puerto Ricans. I had been in upper Manhattan before on one hundred and twenty fifth street, between 7th and 8th avenue, to see someone known as the "Hardest Working Man in Show Business" dance on stage. I had never seen anyone slide across the floor from one end to the other on one leg. After I told Frederick Steinberg I had been to the Apollo to see James Brown, he said white folks were afraid to come to Harlem at night for fear of being mugged and robbed, but when the "God-Father of Soul" came to town, the Negros would allow Caucasians to see the show, just so long as they didn't stick around after it was over!

Me and Freddy were sitting at the front of the restaurant with a view of the projects. I wondered if Negro people liked Japanese food because the place was filled with a lot of white kids like me.

"Why did you bring me here?" I said, putting my overcoat and schoolbooks on top of the chair beside me. "I thought we were going to eat some steaks?"

"We are," he said with a big smile. "I brought you here because I was born and raised in those projects across the street and Mama Sung cooks the best chicken I ever ate."

"Wait a minute, you were born across the street?" I said surprised.

"Yep," he said proudly. "Most people think I'm white, but my father is Jewish, and my mother is black. I'm not ashamed of who I am, but I try to keep it on the down low because white people would start freaking out if they knew I was really black."

"What do you think would happen if they did find out?"

"I would have to start selling watermelons in the cafeteria at school, so everybody would think I haven't forgotten that I'm still a Negro!" he said jokingly.

I shook my head and smiled. Freddy had this sense of humor that could make anyone start laughing.

"Rabbi Jacob knows I'm black, because him and my father grew up together, and the reason he treats me the way he does."

"So, that's what you meant about being born on the other side of the tracks?"

"Yeah, but I don't let it bother me. My father taught me to look at what's inside a person not what's outside."

I suddenly understood why Frederick Steinberg decided to stop David Cross and Billy Blocker from taking my money today in school. "You're a good friend, Freddy," I said feeling grateful I had met someone like him.

"So are you, little brother, and I'm glad to make your acquaintance," he said winking his eye.

I picked up the menu and was amazed. "They've got everything from steak and potatoes to pancakes and waffles," I said impressed.

"Not only that, I think there's a black man in the kitchen who cooks because this place has the best chicken I ever ate."

"May I take your order please, Mister Freddy?" said the Japanese lady with silver and black hair.

The waitress was about fifty years old and wore a white uniform, black apron with pockets, and white shoes. Her hair was tied into a ponytail with chopsticks holding it in place.

"We'll have two T-Bone Steaks with baked potatoes, some macaroni and cheese, and some toasted Italian bread," he said. "Oh yeah and some pink lemonade."

"How do you want your steaks cooked?" she asked, writing everything down.

"Well done. And one more thing, Mama Sung. let me have two orders of fried chicken to go when we leave.

The waitress walked away.

Freddy looked at me. "I want you to taste this chicken when you get home because it's outta sight."

After overhearing the conversation between Rabbi Jacob and Freddy inside the men's room, I decided to find out what Freddy thought about gay people. "Can I ask you a question?" I said, leaning back against the chair.

"Sure you can. What's up?"

"Everybody says gay people won't ever go to Heaven because God doesn't like them. I was wondering how you felt?"

"You are what you are because God made you that way!" he said looking me straight in the eye. "And He did it to see if you could handle it."

I was very surprised by his answer and quickly sat up in my seat to listen to someone who seemed to know more about God than I did.

"And let me slide this up under you," he continued like a motivational speaker, "God uses people all the time, but He never uses them for the wrong reasons. Some of the most successful people in the world are just like you because God wants to show everybody that He's the one who judges people."

Freddy took a moment to see if I was paying attention, and it seemed as if God was talking to me through him.

"Everybody knows the Rabbi's son, Mathew, is gay but Mathew doesn't care. You know why?"

"No."

"Because he's a cheer leader and dances with the girls at the basketball games. Now if he was ashamed of himself, he wouldn't do it. It's not about what kind of a person is inside the human being, Mister Shumsky, it's about what kind of a human being is inside the person. Be yourself and don't worry about what people think. Just worry about what God thinks!"

My mom and dad had never talked to me the way Freddy just did, and I immediately felt like I wasn't this sinful person God disliked so much. "Thanks, Freddy, for making me feel like I'm not a queer," I said happily.

"Anytime, little brother, anytime."

I looked out the window at the projects feeling like God brought me a real friend just when I needed one.

"What are you going to do after you graduate?" I said, leaning back against my chair again.

"Be a fireman like my old man," he said biting his nails. "They make good money and have to stay in shape all the time, so that's what I'm going to do. What about you?"

"I thought about being a photographer like my dad because he taught me a lot about cameras."

"Your old man's a photographer?"

"No, he's a policeman, but taking pictures is one of his hobbies."

"Taking pictures is cool, but you should do what your father does and be a cop," he said spitting what was in his mouth on the floor.

"Why?"

"Because there's not a lot of good cops in New York City and you would make a good one."

"My dad is a good cop and so is my grandfather."

"Yeah, but New York needs a lot of good cops, not just a few."

I looked at Freddy wondering if I should take his advice because he seemed to know me better than I did myself. "Everybody in my family is a cop and I know that's what my dad wants me to be."

"Then go with the flow," he said leaning back in his chair. "And now that you're going to go to karate school, I want you to always remember how you felt today when David Cross and Billy Blocker tried to take your money."

Freddy's serious facial expression made me smile.

"I want you to promise me you're gonna kick ass and take name," he said like a drill sergeant. "You promise?"

"I promise," I said feeling as though my life was about to change.

THIRTY THREE

I DON'T KNOW if my mom had anything to do with Phillip Cross not pressing any charges against Freddy for hitting his son, but Rabbi Jacob took Freddy off suspension two days later and let him go back on the weightlifting team to compete in the school tournaments again. Freddy was very happy. So was I. I told Freddy I didn't want to be an assistant on the weightlifting team because I wanted to go to the karate school and keep my promise about kicking ass and taking names. Freddy gave me a big smile as if he knew I wouldn't let him down.

I bought a white karate suit and a brand-new pair of white basketball shoes to go with my outfit. I don't know what made me buy tennis shoes, since everyone practiced martial arts techniques on their bare feet, but I decided to buy them with the belief they might bring me some good luck.

The first three months at the school were torture. All I did was exercise just to tone up my muscles without learning anything about the martial arts itself. My karate instructor, Mister Toomey, was very strict and made sure everyone performed all the calisthenics the way he showed us. I was determined to be his best student because I remembered the feeling I had when David and Billy tried to take my money, and I felt powerless to stop them. I even stayed after class to continue practicing the different drills we had to do. By the fifth month I had mastered the art of kicking anything that was short or tall, as well as spin around on either foot and strike my opponent with the left or right heel of my other foot. Mister Toomey also showed me how to jump up in the air and snap kick my opponent with great force and then land on my feet. Because of my rapid development, I was selected to compete in the Amateur

Brown Belt competition on Saturday morning against another student in the same school. Freddy said he would be at the karate match to watch me perform.

THIRTY FOUR

FREDDY MET ME on Saturday morning at school about an hour before I was to compete in the tournament. He was wearing a grey sweatshirt with our school emblem, blue jeans, white basketball shoes, and a black Yarmulke on his head. I was dressed in dungarees, wool shirt, and the same type of tennis shoes Freddy wore. Freddy gave up on trying to get a date with Katheryn, after she said her boyfriend was a student at the karate school. As me and Freddy passed the registration office, we saw Katheryn arguing with someone at her desk. He wore a white karate suit, brown belt, (which is one degree below a black belt), and black rubber thongs on his feet.

"Listen, Katheryn, I'm sorry about what happened, but I was drunk, and she came on to me," he said standing at the desk.

His name was Willian McDuffie. He was a seventeen-year-old Caucasian and stood five feet eight-inches tall. His physique wasn't as well developed as Freddy's muscles, but he still had a nice-looking body. I had never seen him in any karate matches, but I heard he won gold and silver medals in a lot of tournaments.

"It doesn't matter because I saw you kissing her like the two of you were in love," she said. "Now if you'll excuse me, I have work to do."

Katheryn was clothed in the same sweatshirt she said belonged to her brother but wouldn't tell Freddy his name. William McDuffie attempted to sit on the front edge of the desk. Katheryn jumped from her chair and began walking away. William immediately grabbed her arm. "Listen Kathy," he said holding her tightly, "just give me a chance to…"

"Let go of my arm," she said angrily.

Freddy walked into the office. I followed Freddy but stopped at the door. I wanted to warn him about William being a brown belt, but I knew Freddy wasn't going to let that stop him from coming to the aid of a girl he had been infatuated with from the first time he saw her.

Freddy put his hands into his pants pockets. "Excuse me, but I was wondering if you could let the lady help me get signed up for the karate class?" he said politely.

"Listen, little Jewish boy, can't you see she's busy?" William said arrogantly. "Why don't you have a seat and when I'm finished talking, you can sign up then?"

I couldn't see Freddy's face when William called him a little Jewish boy, but I knew Freddy wasn't smiling.

"Why don't you let the lady's arm go so she can give me an application to fill out while I wait?" he said calmly.

"Why don't you find someplace to sit down before I break every bone in your body," said William releasing Katheryn's wrist and pushing Freddy away in the face with the same hand.

Freddy almost fell as he stumbled backwards. William walked around the desk towards Freddy. Freddy raised his fists like a prize fighter and attempted to hit William in the face with a stiff left jab.

William side-stepped Freddy's jab and kicked him directly on the kneecap with the heel of his right foot. Freddy loss his balance and stagger backwards again. William turned sideways and gave Freddy another kick to the stomach with the same foot. Freddy went sailing headfirst into the wall by the office door and looked as if he was about to faint. William then stomped his left foot on top of Freddy's stomach. Freddy suddenly folded up like a paper bag and held his stomach like he was in real bad pain.

Katheryn picked up the receiver on the phone at her desk and started dialing numbers as fast as she could. I ran towards William and was going to push him away from Freddy, but William saw me coming and quickly punched me in the chest. I instantly backed up and started gasping for air.

"Listen, you little sissy, you better learn how to mind your own business or I'm going to break every bone in your little body too," William growled.

I don't know why, but ever since David Cross called me and Freddy a sissy that day in school, hearing that word made me very angry. I managed to recover from William's punch and stared at him with my hands on my hips. "YOUR DADDY'S A SISSY AND SO ARE YOU. YOU FAGGOT!" I said boldly.

William looked as if he couldn't believe I had the nerve to insult him and ran towards me. I turned around like I was going to run out of the door. William started running faster. I turned around, jumped in the air, and caught him by surprise with a snap kick to the bridge of his nose. He quickly realized he had been caught off guard with me pretending to run out the door and tried to regain his composure after being struck in the face. I rushed towards him and was about to jump up and kick him again, but he dropped to the floor and used his right foot to kick my legs from under me. I hit the floor like a ton of bricks. William stood up, snatched my right leg so that I couldn't stand, and started stomping my ribcage with his right foot while holding my leg. Every time he stomped down on my ribs, it felt like a herd of cattle stampeding across my whole body. I managed to grab his right foot after the fourth time and started biting his big toe because all he had on his feet were rubber thongs. He immediately released my leg and tried to yank his foot from out of my mouth, but I held on to his big toe like a Pitbull. As William attempted to yank his foot out of my mouth he fell to the floor. I hurriedly stood up on my feet. William managed to take a karate stance, but the pain in his right foot made him put all his weight on the left side. I charged towards him and leaped into the air again. This time I kicked him square in the face with both feet. William did a somersault over the desk like he had been hit with a cannon ball. I could hear him groaning in pain while lying on the floor in front of Katheryn. Freddy managed to stand up and walked unsteadily to the chairs by the door. After leaping in the air and kicking William with both feet, I land on my stomach. I immediately jumped up on top of the desk and then down on William's stomach with all my weight. William curled up like a baby in a four-wheel carriage, after I bounced off his body like it was a trampoline. The office door was surrounded by people looking inside to see what all the commotion was about.

The manager came rushing through the crowd and into the office. "You want to tell me what in tarnation is going on here, Miss Cross?" he said to Katheryn.

The manager was about thirty years old and skinny. He wore a plaid shirt, black tie, and floppy hairstyle. He reminded me of Mick Jagger the rock and roll star.

Katheryn was still overcome with shock as she spoke. "This all started because of Billy McDuffie," She said glancing at me, while William continued to lay on the floor behind the desk. "Mr. Shumsky had a fight with Billy because Billy kicked Mr. Shumsky's friend over there sitting by the door."

The manager looked at me and Freddy. He couldn't see William, but he could hear someone moaning in pain and strolled around the desk to see who it was. "What are you doing on the floor, Mr. McDuffie?" he said helping William to stand up.

I walked over to Freddy and lifted him by the arm. I knew he wasn't feeling swelled. I couldn't see William, because he was still lying on the floor, but I knew he was feeling a lot worse than Freddy. I also knew he would think twice before calling me a sissy again.

Freddy put his arm around my shoulder. "I guess that makes us even, little brother," he said happily.

"What do you mean?"

"You saved my butt from Katheryn's boyfriend, just like I stopped David Cross and Billy Blocker from taking your money."

"Yep, that makes us even," I said grinning.

William McDuffie rose to his feet while holding his stomach.

"You know this isn't over dude," he said angrily.

I was about to challenge William again, but Freddy kept his arm around my shoulder. "He's just talking little brother, because his pride is hurt," Freddy stated quickly. "You really changed his spark plugs with those snap kicks and believe me, he doesn't want to see you no time soon because his big toe looks like a potato from Idaho!"

The crowd at the door laughed because of the way Freddy rhymed the words, Big Toe and Idaho. I was happy Freddy hadn't lost his sense of humor.

Freddy turned around to look at William. "I guess you thought my friend couldn't fight, but you learned your lesson after he took one bite!" Freddy said continuing to be poetic.

As me and Freddy walked out the office, the crowd made a path like we were movie stars on the red carpet. After we reached the men's locker room, I looked at Freddy. "I think Katheryn's brother is David Cross," I said suddenly.

Freddy unwrapped his arm from around my shoulder and stared at me.

"Didn't you hear the manager call her, Miss Cross?" I said, massaging my chest where William McDuffie first punched me. "And remember when she told you the sweatshirt, she had on belonged to her brother, but wouldn't tell you his name?"

Freddy suddenly frowned. "She'll probably hate me for the rest of my life, if she ever finds out I slapped her brother."

"HEY, MISTER SHUMSKY!" Katheryn yelled as she rushed towards me.

Me and Freddy turned around. I thought she was going to thank me for beating up her boyfriend, but she looked at Freddy.

"You never told me your name when we first met."

"It's Frederick Steinberg."

"I just want to say thank you, Mister Steinberg, for trying to make Billy stop bothering me, and I'm really sorry about him hitting you," she said regretfully.

"That's okay, I would have done the same thing for anybody. And you don't have to call me, Mr. Steinberg. My name's Freddy."

Katheryn looked at me. "I've never seen anyone fight the way you do, Mr. Shumsky," she said with admiration. "I'm sure Freddy is glad you two are friends."

"He's my best friend," I said proudly.

"Can I ask you a question? Is David Cross your brother?" Freddy said curiously.

Katheryn noticed the school emblem on Freddy's sweatshirt. "I see you go to the same school as he does," she said amused. "Do you know him?"

"We've never really met, but we did run into each other at school one day."

"Well, I just want to say thank you once more," she said again.

"Can I ask you another question?" he said putting both hands into his pants pockets.

Katheryn waited for Freddy to ask the question.

"Will you let me take you to lunch tomorrow?"

Katheryn looked at Freddy for a long time before she spoke. "You certainly are persistent," she smiled.

"Does that mean, yes'?"

"I go to lunch at eleven o'clock tomorrow. Can you be here?"

"No problem. I just hope I don't run into your boyfriend again, since I know he doesn't like me and Thomas."

"He's not my boyfriend anymore," she said distastefully, "and the way your friend, Mr. Shumsky, fights I don't think anyone around here is going to mess with you, including Billy."

Katheryn went back to her office. I won the Amateur Brown Belt Competition in front of two hundred karate students. I also wore the tennis shoes while competing against my opponents. Freddy was very proud. So was I, and delighted I let him convince me to take karate lessons so I wouldn't be afraid of people like David, Billy, and William.

THIRTY FIVE

300 YEARS after the death of Jesus Christ, the Armenians were the first people to adopt Christianity as their official religion while living in Turkey and under the rulership of a Muslim Government known as the "Ottoman Empire." A civil war between the Turks and the Islamic Government started taking place at the beginning of the 16th Century for political and social reasons but mainly because of their different religious beliefs. In 1915, 1.5 million civilians were massacred by the government in what was believed to be a preconceived plan by the empire to exterminate the Armenian civilization! That genocide went somewhat unnoticed by many of the other countries around the globe, due to the fact "World War One" was being fought across several continents at the same time the Turkish People were struggling for their own independence.

A rebel group composed of two men and a woman, and known as the "Armenian Revolutionary Federation," began their struggle against the Ottoman Empire in 1890. The freedom fighters started assassinating government officials they believed were corrupted politicians working in the interest of the Muslim Regime. A plot to eliminate Talaat Pasha from office, who was Prime Minister of the Empire at the time, was unsuccessful because one of the assassins was apprehended before the mission was completed. The remaining two insurgents fled to Antioch with hopes of finding refuge with the clergymen who worked in the famous cathedral that was once a synagogue. Their names were Giro and Selma Yagman.

The identity of the twin couple had been a well-kept secret in Armenia, until the governmental authorities found a photograph of them as teenagers living in the northern hills of Turkey. The photograph was discovered at the farm where the Yagman Family lived, after government soldiers raided their home in a desperate search for anyone connected to the Revolutionary Federation and executed Mr. and Mrs. Yagman for refusing to reveal the whereabouts of their two children. With just an old picture of Giro and Selma, and the fact they had red hair, the authorities were waiting for any information leading to their new location.

The Ottoman Empire finally received news Giro and Salma were hiding in Antioch and living inside the cathedral. Two specially trained soldiers from the Ottoman Empire went to Antioch in search of the Yagman Twins. On August 13, 1938, both soldiers dressed themselves in civilian clothes and waited for the rebel leader and his sister to show up at the house of worship. The two officers were armed with tommy guns and sitting in a green unmarked vehicle parked 50 yards away from the entrance. On the dashboard was the old photograph of Giro and Selma as teenagers with red hair. There was also a set of binoculars on the dashboard with the photograph.

THIRTY SIX

ROBERT SHUMSKY couldn't wait to tell Fatima about a plan he put together on paper, so she could see a step-by-step formula that would guaranty the Ta'if Dancers a successful career once they came to America. All he had to do was persuade the young starlet to accompany him to the church this morning and explain everything to her privately. That way it would be easier to convince the superstar to go along with the plan after she was away from everyone else.

Robert and Rosemary slept in the same guest room, but in separate beds. The date was August 13, 1938. The time was 6:54 a.m. Robert had just finished bathing and sat on his sister's bed, dressed in underwear and drying his hair with a towel. There was a dark suit, white shirt and black tie, spread across his own bed. Beside the suit were black shoes and a Stetson Hat worn by Orthodox Jews. Next to the hat was his camera.

"Rosy, I want you to ask Fatima if she would like to go with us to visit the synagogue this morning," he said, deciding not to explain why he wanted Fatima to come along.

Rosemary wore a thin white cotton dress and sat on the edge of her bed holding a hand mirror and brushing her hair. A pair of white flat heel shoes were on the floor beside the bed. Her mouth was painted with red lipstick. There was a white bonnet with ribbon on the bed she intended to wear to keep the sunlight away from her sensitive skin.

"It isn't a synagogue anymore, Bobby, it's a church because Paul changed it after he became a Christian," she said, admiring herself in the mirror. "And what's the big deal with me asking her, why don't you ask her yourself?"

"Because it wouldn't be polite for me knock on her door," he replied. "Just go ask her if she wouldn't mind tagging along because I want to take some pictures of us together before you and I go back home."

Rosemary placed the mirror on the bed, put on her shoes, and walked out the door. Fifteen minutes later, she was back in the room. Robert was fully dressed and putting film inside the camera.

"Fatima said she would go, but she also said she wanted to come back early and be with her girlfriends before they leave with Abu Bakr," said Rosemary.

Robert smiled. Hopefully Fatima and her girlfriends would be making America their home, he told himself.

THIRTY SEVEN

THE SYNAGOGUE CONVERTED into a Christian Cathedral was located on the outskirts of Antioch, one mile east of the Mediterranean Sea. It was a large building capable of occupying 250 guests. Residents of the city and tourists from all parts of the globe came dressed in their best apparel to commemorate the "Resurrection of Jesus Christ" on the third day of his "Crucifixion," as well as pay tribute to a structure that was once a Jewish Temple. Because of the enormous crowd of spectators, the priest in charge of conducting church services, held three separate sessions.

Robert, Rosemary, and Fatima arrived at the cathedral on horseback and without bodyguards. Fatima was dressed in a one-piece hijab, silk scarf over her head, and leather sandals. They were waiting with a host of other visitors for the second service to start. Robert decided to take pictures of Fatima and Rosemary while they waited. The first snapshots were of them standing together with their arms around each other.

"Take off your bonnet, Rosy," said Robert with his Stetson Hat on.

Rosemary untied the ribbon beneath her chin, took off the bonnet, and shook out her hair. Robert removed his hat and wiped the perspiration from his brow with the back of his hand. The green unmarked vehicle with the soldiers inside was facing the church entrance and camouflaged amongst the trees. The tall muscular officer wearing a white shirt and no tie, and sitting on the passenger's side, noticed Rosemary while scanning the crowd with binoculars. He adjusted the lens to get a closer look at the female with red hair. She didn't resemble Selma because their facial features were different, but the man taking pictures also had red hair, which made him want to know who these twins were and if they could be of use in helping to find the real Giro and Selma.

"Take a look at these two people with red hair," he said giving the binoculars to his comrade.

The short overweight officer behind the wheel took the binoculars and looked at the twin couple.

"What do you think?" asked the muscular officer.

The driver also wore a white shirt and no tie. "They are not the ones we want, but they might be able to help us to find the real Giro and Selma," he said giving the binoculars back to the passenger and turning on the ignition.

The passenger took one of the machine guns off the backseat and placed it on his lap. The vehicle sped towards the church.

After taking several pictures of Rosemary and Fatima, Robert gave the camera to his sister. He held his hat with one hand and put his arm around Fatima's shoulder. "Now take some of us," he instructed Rosemary.

Rosemary gave her bonnet to Robert, backed away from the handsome couple, and took pictures of her brother and the beautiful belly dancer. Fatima noticed the green automobile racing towards Rosemary like a bat out of hell and commenced to yell. "ROSE MARY, LOOK OUT BEHIND YOU!" screamed Fatima.

The automobile was traveling at sixty miles an hour. Rosemary turned around and almost dropped the camera as the green four door sedan came to a screeching halt, just inches away from where she stood. Rosemary stared at the men inside the car. Robert and Fatima rushed towards Rosemary. Both soldiers exited the vehicle like policemen. The muscular man with the gun marched to the front of the car and pointed his weapon at Rosemary. "What is your name?" he said sternly.

"Hey, what are you doing?" said Robert with his arm around his sister's shoulder.

"We want the both of you two to come with us," insisted the

overweight man.

"For what?" said Robert angrily.

"We will explain later, but right now you need to get into the car," ordered the man with the weapon.

"Bobby, what are they doing?" said Rosemary, terrified.

"I don't know, but we're not going anywhere," he assured her.

The overweight man quickly grabbed Robert's arm. "Listen, you filthy American! Either you come with us or get shot," he said holding the foreigner as if he was a criminal.

Robert snatched his arm away from the bully. "You can't force us to go anywhere," he said gallantly. "I insist you take us to the Foreign Embassy right now."

Before either of the two soldiers could react, Fatima spoke to them in Arabic. The soldier with the weapon laughed. "We do not have to talk to any government officials, we are from the Ottoman Empire and can do whatever we want," he said continuing to point his weapon at the twins.

Fatima became enraged and wished she had a tommy gun.

The overweight driver released the American's arm and retrieved the other Tommy Gun on the backseat of the automobile. "Both of you get in the car," he demanded, pulling back on the lever and putting his finger on the trigger.

Robert stepped in front of his sister. "We're not going anywhere until we see some identification," he said courageously. Robert looked at Fatima. "Fatima, go and get your father."

Without hesitation, the muscular soldier struck Robert across the mouth with the butt of his gun. Robert dropped his hat and Rosemary's bonnet and fell to his knees with blood-stained teeth. He tried to stand up. The pain was unbearable. Rosemary charged towards the muscular soldier. "You leave him alone," she said dropping the camera and pushing him away from her brother.

The tall soldier yanked the lever back on his weapon, pointed it at Rosemary, and pulled the trigger. Four bullets erupted from the gun, hitting Rosemary in the chest. She fell to the dirt with her eyes opened.

" ROSY!" Robert cried as he crawled towards his sister.

The citizens and tourists turned towards the sound of gunfire and looked with horror at the girl laying on the ground and her body riddled with bullets.

The overweight driver looked at his comrade. "We need to take him back with us alive," he cautioned.

Fatima stared at Rosemary wondering what to do. The driver tried to pull Robert from the dead corpse. Robert grabbed his weapon. They both struggled to get control of the gun. Female tourists began screaming at the top of their lungs as they watched the two men tussle with each other. Robert pushed him in the direction of the vehicle. The driver lost his balance, hit his head on the bumper, and was becoming unconscious.

Robert attempted to stand up with the weapon in his hand but was hit in the back of his skull by the other soldier with a Tommy Gun. Robert fell to the ground once more. He didn't lose consciousness, but the impact from the gun against the bony framework of his head, resulted in him releasing the weapon and becoming completely dazed.

The soldier snatched the back of Robert's collar and dragged him to the passenger's side. Fatima rushed to the Tommy Gun beside the unconscious soldier. "Let him go," she said pointing the gun at the soldier holding Robert by the collar.

The muscular man with no hair on his face looked at Fatima and released Robert's shirt. He pointed his firearm at Robert Shumsky's head. "Put the gun down, or I will kill your friend," he threatened.

Fatima calmly pulled the trigger. Seven rounds of bullets ejected from the machine gun in rapid succession before the soldier knew what hit him. The first three shells penetrated his shirt like a sewing machine needle. The last four bullets hit him with such fury, he died before dropping his weapon and falling next to Robert.

Fatima turned to the overweight man on the ground. He was still unconscious. She immediately sprayed him with eight shells across the body. The fat man bounced up and down like a basketball, as the armored casings pierced his carcass like poison darts. The crowd began scattering away like frightened animals, after witnessing Fatima execute the overweight soldier in cold blood.

"We need to leave," said Fatima helping Robert to stand up.

Robert stared at his sister and commenced to cry like a helpless child.

"Robert, you have to pull yourself together," Fatima pleaded. "We have leave before some more of them get here."

"But we didn't do anything," he sobbed. "As soon as they get here, we'll tell them what happened."

"Robert, these people are from the Ottoman Empire," she said opening the door on the passenger's side. "When they find out what happened, they will send more soldiers to kill us." Fatima tossed the Tommy Gun on the floor in front of the seat. "Do you know how to drive?"

"Yeah," he replied wiping away his tears.

"Put Rosemary in the backseat and let us go tell my father," she said, sitting in the seat.

Robert hoisted Rosemary off the ground, opened the back door, and rested her body in the backseat. He ran around the front end and jumped behind the wheel. The green automobile raced down the road, leaving the camera on the ground near the two dead soldiers.

THIRTY EIGHT

"BOTH OF YOU HAVE TO LEAVE RIGHT AWAY!" said Miriam sitting at the head of the dining room table. Fatima sat between her parents on the right side of the wealthy widow. Mustafa and Robert were on the left. Abu Bakr and The Ta'if Dancers were upstairs in their guest rooms.

"Fatima, you must go to America with Robert, but first you must disguise yourself as his sister and dye your hair red," Miriam continued. "No one knows she's dead right now, so you will have no problem leaving as Rosemary Shumsky."

Fatima and Robert were surprised by her proposal to go to the United States, rather than him returning alone. "But what about my sister, what's going to happen to her?" he said sitting on the edge of the chair.

"I will see she gets a proper burial," responded Miriam, "but you must leave before I have to bury you too!"

Fatima thought about returning to Ta'if with the dance group. "Is there a way for me to take the blame without Robert being involved?" inquired Fatima sympathetically.

Miriam fell back against the chair. "Probably not," she said frankly. "The government is going to be searching for the people who killed the soldiers, once they develop those pictures from his camera."

"May I say something, if you do not mind?" said Mustafa looking at his sister.

Miriam nodded her head. "If you wish."

"I believe that God has a plan for you and Robert, little cousin," he said turning his attention to Fatima, "and meeting him at the marketplace was not just a coincidence."

"What kind of plan?" said Fatima as though she believed him.

"I'm not sure, but I'm certain that God has a plan because of our conversation about me being a eunuch and your belief that being gay is a matter of choice."

"Well, my dear brother, that does not tell her very much," commented Miriam.

"I believe it does," interjected Omar. "Fatima taught me to accept her for what she is and not for what I hoped she would be." Omar placed his arm around his daughter's shoulder and kissed her cheek. "Just remember your mother and I love you very much and maybe you will have a child and learn to accept them as they are."

Tears fell from Fatima's eye. "I love you father," she said resting her head against his chest, "and you too mother."

"Now that we know what must be done, let us get started," said Miriam rising from the chair.

"Fatima lifted her head from her father's chest," Will I ever see my mother and father again?" she asked Miriam.

"I will see what I can do, but I will make sure you stay in contact with them while you are in America. "

Fatima said goodbye to Abu Bakr and the Ta'if Dancers and left for America as Robert Shumsky sister. Meanwhile, the Arab Government circulated wanted posters of Robert and Fatima throughout all Syria, along with a $25,000 reward for any information leading to their capture and conviction.

THIRTY NINE

ROBERT BERNARD SHUMSKY introduced Fatima to his mother and father, and to his grandfather who was a retired police officer. The retired officer's name was Thomas Emilio Shumsky. Robert told everyone what happened to Rosemary and how Fatima saved his life by shooting the soldiers after they murdered his sister. He continued explaining that the Arab Government was searching for him and Fatima in connection with the soldiers being killed and why it was decided to bury Rosemary in Antioch and allow Fatima to use her passport to come to the United States.

Mr. Theodore Shumsky was a narcotics detective at the 27th precinct in New York City. After being seriously wounded by some drug dealers in the Greenwich Village area of lower Manhattan, he promised his wife he would take a desk job, so she wouldn't have to worry about him putting his life in danger anymore. Mrs. Alice Shumsky was a registered nurse, but retired, and spent much of her time supervising the P.T.A. Meetings in the community as Chairman of the Board. Everyone in the Shumsky Family were heartbroken after hearing the news about Rosemary being killed the way Robert described it. Theodore was especially devastated because he had high hopes of his daughter becoming the first female police officer in New York City. Now all was lost, and he began thinking about leaving the desk and returning to the streets of New York City where he felt he belonged and stop criminals like the two soldiers who murdered his daughter.

To show their appreciation for saving Robert's life, Mr. and Mrs. Shumsky agreed to tell neighbors and friends Rosemary died in a car accident and let Fatima continue to use their daughter's first name, but changed the last name to Kissinger, so everyone wouldn't be suspicious about Fatima having the same last name as the person who just so happened to die accidently. Robert Shumsky also decided to abandon the idea of making Fatima the famous dancer he had in mind, since it was important her face be kept out of the public eye.

FORTY

ROBERT AND FATIMA were married one year after she came to America. The wedding was held in a Jewish Synagogue. The guests assumed Fatima was Jewish because of her last name being Kissinger. However, she became Rosemary Shumsky anyway, after getting married. Becoming a Jewish wife did not prevent Fatima from continuing to practice the religion of Islam in the privacy of her home to avoid any gossip from friends and neighbors. Robert knew better than to try and change his wife's religious beliefs just because she was married to him and resolved not to interfere with anything she did as a Muslim, even though they were married under the Jewish Laws. The following year, Robert graduated from the academy and was assigned to work at the same station as his father. Fatima was happy about her husband following in the footsteps of his family and looking forward to becoming a simple housewife and having children. That was until Thomas Emilio Shumsky was born on August 12, 1940. Which happened to be the same month and day she was born. Robert chose the name, Thomas Emilio Shumsky, for his son in memory of his grandfather being the first policeman in the family, along with the decision his wife would be disallowed to teach their son anything about the Islamic Faith because he was being raised under the banner of Judaism. Fatima believed the only reason Robert married her was to have more policemen in the Shumsky family and was really no different than King Azad, both of whom had this absurd viewpoint about women being nothing more than a piece of furniture to be used when it suited them. Fatima concluded being just a housewife was not in her best interest and decided not to have any more children and use the identity of Robert's sister to finish law school, since her domineering husband was acting like a jerk. Two years later, she passed the bar examination with flying colors and became a public defender. Five years after that, she was one of the ten top district attorneys in New York City. At the age of 49, she was sitting on the bench as a Superior Court Judge and exercising the kind of judicial power the average woman in America only dreamed about. The only thing she wished she could change was pretending to be Jewish. However, living in the United States taught her something very important. Real respect comes from what you do, not who you are!

FORTY ONE

DETERMINED to succeed in a judicial system predominately run by the male species, Fatima used her beauty and charm just like she did in the old days while living in Ta'if to climb the ladder of success. Men in America were no different than they were anywhere else in the world, with insatiable appetites for money and power, which Fatima took advantage of quite easily. However, her road to prominence wasn't without its trials and tribulations. There were numerous attempts by the district attorney's office to remove her from the bench because she ran her courtroom unlike other judges and dismissed criminal cases when the defender's rights were violated. This attitude about following rules and regulations stemmed from the time she had to shoot two government soldiers because they refused to follow protocol by not taking Robert and his sister to the Foreign Embassy before arresting them.

To prevent being removed from the bench, Fatima leveled the playing by taking photographs of the men she had sexual relationships with and tape recording of those who made arrangements on the telephone to meet with her privately. One of her clients was Arnold Martin, Senior Member of the Judicial Counsel. Mr. Martin was a married man with two sons in college. After being shown pictures of himself in hotel rooms, he did everything she asked. Including that she would not be removed from her position as Superior Court Judge. The other affair was with Phillip Cross. Rosemary met Phillip through her husband when she and Robert first came to the United States. Robert took her to the Department of Immigration to get the credentials she needed to be the fictitious Rosemary Kissinger. It wasn't until she went with her son to Antioch and Phillip helped her get safely back into the United States that their affair began. Which didn't last very long, due to Phillip Cross being bisexual and not a real lady's man.

FORTY TWO

AFTER 28 YEARS IN AMERICA, Fatima gave the family name an honorable place in the criminal justice system while pretending to be a United States Citizen. The only thing she deeply regretted was a marriage not working out as she had hoped. There were times when she felt like walking away from a profession that didn't matter as much as being able to raise a child the way a mother is supposed to do. There was also the fact she and Robert failed in trying to balance their personal careers along with a marriage requiring more commitment than they were willing to make. Here they were, 28 years later, living in the same house as strangers, with a child who turned out to be something they never expected. Thomas Emilio Shumsky showed signs of having feminine characteristics as he got older. Instead of interacting with other children, he isolated himself, wishing he didn't feel uncomfortable around other boys his age. Robert Shumsky decided to take his son to see a shrink, who diagnosed Thomas as being introverted, which of course was perfectly normal for adolescents going through puberty, as the psychiatrist tried to explain to a very unhappy father. Believing there was absolutely nothing that could be done, Robert Shumsky went through an emotional tailspin with believing God was punishing him for being more devoted to a job than his Jewish faith.

Fatima did her best to accept Emilio as he was, but her understanding as a Muslim regarding homosexuality was that Allah was still going to punish Emilio even though he was born the way he was. Knowing Robert had forbidden her to teach him anything about the Islamic faith, she broke a cardinal rule and taught Emilio how to read the Holy Quran, as well as speak Arabic, hoping it might help him avoid being punished like the people of Sodom and

Gomorrah. Emilio was ten years old when she began teaching him how to speak Arabic and read the Holy Quran, with a reminder not to tell his father what they were doing. The young novice mastered the dialect very quickly and memorized the entire Quran by age 12, because the verses were chanted when recited and Emilio treated the scriptures as if they were lyrics to a song. Fatima was both happy and extremely proud in what he had accomplished in such a short time. What she didn't expect was that he made her reexamine what she thought she knew about predestination, or "Qadar," as referred to in the Arabic language.

Emilio was sitting on the living room floor with the Quran in his lap and decided one afternoon to ask his mother about something he didn't understand. "Does Allah know what we're going to do before we do it?" he said inquisitively.

Fatima was seated on the rug in front of her son. "Yes," she replied with certainty. "Why do you ask such a question?"

"Because I don't understand how predestination works."

"Can you be more specific?"

"If Allah knows what I'm going to do before I do it, then I really don't have the free will to do what I want, because He already knows what I'm going to do!"

Fatima had wrestled with this question as a child herself and concluded that although no one knows how this mystery works, does not mean they are deprive of having the free will to make their own decisions.

"Allah tells us in the Holy Quran not to commit sins, and when a person does commit a sin to ask God for forgiveness. Is this true?"

"Yes," said Emilio staring intently at his mother.

"And the reason He tells us to ask for forgiveness, is so He can help us to stop doing the things that are sinful. Is this true?"

"Yes," said Emilio again.

"Although Muslim believes Allah already knows our future, does not mean we cannot make our own choices because Allah says everyone has the power to resist temptation with prayer. You, and only you, are the one who decides whether or not you will go to heaven or hell, not Allah."

Fatima was hoping her son was able to accept the explanation she offered, despite the fact she never understood how predestination worked herself.

"So, if a person does something they believe is right, will Allah still punish them because it was wrong from the beginning?" he asked, still puzzled.

Fatima thought about why she decided to become a prostitute in Ta'if and believed it was necessary to make enough money to pay for her family's freedom from a prison camp. However, becoming a prostitute under the pretense it was necessary to reach the position of a Superior Court Judge, did not seem as good a reason as the one made in Ta'if to be a harlot! "I wish I knew the answer to that question myself, Emilio," she said feeling ashamed about becoming a prostitute in America. "Only Allah knows if He will punish us or not because Only He Can Judge Us!"

FORTY THREE

IN THE MONTH OF JULY 1952 , Fatima had not reached the position of Superior Court Judge and received a letter from Miriam Akbar Omar was gravely ill and went to Antioch as Rosemary Shumsky, believing the government had discontinued their search for the people responsible in the death of two soldiers at the church in Antioch 14 years ago. Fatima left without her husband, due to him being shot and having to remain in the hospital until he fully recovered but was able to take Emilio along to see his grandfather. Robert Shumsky had single handedly captured two bank robbers attempting to escape in a stolen vehicle. Because of the courageous officer's heroic act, magazines and newspapers in New York City made his valiant ordeal front page news. Robert was so engulfed with all the attention and publicity, he never noticed his wife and son being absent, while the news reporters showered him with interviews about his own father having the same experience of being shot in the line of duty and capturing the assailants in the Greenwich Village area.

FORTY FOUR

MIRIAM AND MUSTAFA stood at the front door of the mansion watching Fatima and Thomas riding a camel towards the estate. Thomas sat behind his mother with one arm around her waist and pulling a second camel carrying their luggage. Fatima was dressed in a full-length garment like those worn by American women and a scarf around her face for protection from the afternoon sun. Thomas wore a black suit and tie and looked very handsome.

Miriam Akbar was now 47-years old. She was still very beautiful and, needless to say, still very rich. Her estate appeared identically the same as before. The attractive widow never lost step with being the charming hostess she always was. Mustafa had put on a few pounds and didn't resemble the slim and trim merchant he once was, but he did continue to adorn himself with expensive apparel. Mustafa ran towards the two camels in his bare feet. He was covered in a plaid dashiki and long piece of white cloth wrapped around his head like a turban. Fatima pulled the reins on her camel to stop. Mustafa helped his cousin down off the desert animal and then kissed her on both cheeks. Fatima was always so attractive, he reminded himself.

Mustafa looked at Thomas. "And whose adorable child is this, may I ask?"

"This is my son, Thomas," she said proudly.

Mustafa smiled as he lifted Thomas off the camel. "As salaamu alaykum, Thomas," he said extending his right hand.

"Wa alaikum as salaam," replied Thomas shaking hands.

The boy's Arabic is perfect, thought Mustafa releasing the

young man's hand.

Miriam's long black hair was tied into a ponytail and her face without makeup. She was draped in a black hijab and brown leather sandals. Her toenails were colored with white polish. Miriam walked up to Fatima and smiled. "Why did you not tell me you were coming, so I could have arranged for your safe passage?" said Miriam scolding Fatima.

"I wanted to surprise everyone," grinned Fatima.

Miriam spoke Arabic, asking Fatima who was the young dressed in the black suit.

"You can ask him yourself, he speaks Arabic fluently," responded Fatima in Arabic.

Miriam spoke Arabic to Thomas, after which he told her his name, how old he was, and how much he had heard about her and Mustafa from his mother.

"This is a great day for us all," exclaimed Miriam cheerfully. "Your mother and father will be so happy to know they have a grandson. Come let us go inside."

FORTY FIVE

YOUNG THOMAS SHUMSKY never thought he would visit a country where mansions still existed like the one Miriam Akbar owned. The rich widow's residence was exactly like the images in history books at school, and he felt a great sense of pride while admiring the marbled pillars and crystal chandeliers, knowing his mother had lived with the famous Miriam Akbar before coming to the United States.

Omar Muttalib was sleeping. He had suffered a mild stroke and was resting in bed, paralyzed on the left side of his body and unable to use his left hand with any mobility. Aisha was now a frail lady of 63. Her black hair was mixed with grey. She sat in a rocking chair beside her husband weaving a prayer rug together with a needle and thread like she did in the old days when she and her husband sold rugs and other goods to earn a living. Fatima and Thomas held hands as they entered the bedroom. Thomas noticed a strong odor permeating the air like that of a sick patient in a hospital room.

"Hello, Mother," whispered Fatima.

Aisha's expression was of great surprise and happiness upon seeing her daughter for the first time in fourteen years. She placed the rug and sewing kit on the floor and shook her husband by the shoulder. "Omar, Fatima is here," she said elated.

Omar opened his eyes and sat up on his elbows. Dark shadows were beneath his pupils. His face was covered with lines and wrinkles. His hair was as white as snow. He looked every bit of sixty-six. Omar gazed intently at the adolescent holding Fatima's hand. The handsome young man had his mother's face and his father's red hair, thought Omar.

Aisha stood up from her chair as Fatima rushed into her mother's bosom with tears in her eyes. Aisha lavished Fatima's face with kisses. Thomas watched his grandmother begin sobbing like someone overcome with joy. Fatima waved at her son to come towards them "This is your grandson, mother," she said beaming with pride.

"As salaamu alaikum, grandmother," he said politely.

Aisha grinned from ear to ear. Her grandson not only spoke perfect Arabic, but he also had Fatima's forehead and cheekbones, she told herself. "Wa alaikum as salaam," she replied. "May I ask what your name is?"

"Thomas Emilio Shumsky," he boasted.

"It is nice to meet you, Mr. Shumsky. My name is Aisha, and this is your grandfather, Omar," she said pointing to her husband.

"Yes, I know," he said happily. "As salaamu alaikum, Grandfather Omar Muttalib. La ilaha illallah, wa Muhammadur Rasul Allah." (Translated; There is no God but Allah and Muhammad is the Messenger of Allah.)

Omar was impressed by his grandson's command of Arabic and pleased Fatima had taught him the religion of Islam even though he possessed a Jewish name. "Come sit down young man," he said leaning back against the pillow and patting the mattress where he wanted Thomas to sit.

Thomas sat on the bed. Aisha returned to her rocking chair. Fatima took a seat on the bed behind Thomas.

"Miriam told us you sent word that you and Robert were married," Omar began, "did he become a policeman like he said he would?"

"Yes, but he was shot by some bank robbers and is in the hospital," she said sadly. "It is not serious, but the doctor said he cannot leave for a while, which is why he did not come with me and Thomas."

"I am sorry to hear that, and I pray to Allah he makes a full recovery," remarked Omar. "And how are you doing?"

Fatima broke into a smile. "I am one of the youngest district attorneys in New York City," she said hoping he would be impressed, "but I want to be a superior court judge because I can do more than a district attorney."

Omar wasn't surprised his daughter chose a profession which allowed her to express the way she felt, but the question in his mind was how she became an attorney with no formal education in criminal law. "How were you able to do such things, when you have never gone to a law school?" he inquired.

"I used the real Patricia Shumsky's identity to go to law school, since she had already been enrolled at the University in Connecticut," she stated cleverly. "Then I took the test and passed the bar examination."

Omar shook his head. His daughter had the instincts of a survivor no matter what the circumstances were, he thought. Aisha on the other hand wondered if her daughter had belly danced her way into a position of political power. "How is it that you are an attorney, when such things were only meant for men?" frowned Aisha.

"Because things are different in America mother, and women are not just housewives anymore," replied Fatima as though she was in a courtroom.

Everyone's attention was overtaken by the sound of someone knocking on the door. "Come in," said Aisha loudly.

Miriam Akbar's African servant opened the door. He was a frail man with grey hair and still as black as tar. "Dinner is being served," he said politely.

Fatima looked at Aisha. "Mother, would you take Emilio down to the dining hall while I talk to father?"

Aisha and Thomas left the room.

FORTY SIX

THE ROOM WAS QUIET. Fatima sat closer to her father on the bed. "Do you remember when Mustafa said he believed Allah had a plan for me, just before I left for America with Robert?"

"I remember it very well."

"Now I understand what he meant about me feeling differently about gay people, and that Allah had it all planned."

"What do you mean?"

Fatima looked at the sewing kit on the rocking chair in search of a way to explain how she felt. "Thomas is gay!" she said looking at her father again, "and I keep wondering if Allah will still punish him, even though he was born that way."

"And you really believe Thomas did not choose to be what he is?"

"Yes," she replied, peering into his eyes for some sort of empathy.

Omar's facial expression didn't reveal what he was thinking. He sensed his daughter was hoping for some words of comfort and wanted to wait until she finished before he said anything.

"I should have listened to Mustafa a long time ago, but I always believed God would punish gay people no matter what justification they tried to offer."

Fatima's eyes swelled with tears.

"I pray to Allah every night that He be merciful to my son, because Thomas is a good child," she sobbed.

Omar looked at his daughter believing she had learned a great lesson. "Do not worry," he said, his voice filled with compassion. "You must be patient now, Fatima, because it is up to him now to choose the road upon which he will travel."

"Yes, I know," she sighed, "but what kind of life will Emilio have, and how will he be able raise a family like married people do, when his values are different?"

"You gave Thomas something he will value for the rest of his life," he said happily. "You taught him to read the Holy Quran, which is not just a religious book as many people think, but a way of life as you and I both know. If Thomas has learned anything from what the Book of Allah says, then he will be fine."

Omar knew Fatima was still uncertain about Emilio's future and placed his hand upon her cheek the way he did when she was a child and not so sure about things. "Why don't you talk to Mustafa while you still have the chance?" he proposed. "If he gave you some good advice before, I am sure he would not hesitate to do the same now."

Fatima smiled. As always, her father had a way of making things seem like they were not that bad, she thought. "I will go and talk to him right now," she said rising from the bed.

FORTY SEVEN

FATIMA AND MUSTAFA sat at the dining room table alone and were facing each other. Aisha returned to the bedroom to be with Omar. Miriam took Thomas on a tour of the estate. Mustafa held a silver goblet of wine in his hand. Fatima wondered what advice Mustafa would offer and hoping he wouldn't bring up the past and her refusal to listen to him the first time. "I have something to tell you," she said reluctantly.

"And what might that be?" he said, taking a sip of wine.

"You were right about me changing my mind if my own son became a eunuch.

Mustafa placed the cup on the table and leaned back against the chair. "Eunuchs are people who have been castrated. Has Thomas been castrated?"

"No, but he is attracted to men like you are."

"I already know that, little cousin," he said, realizing Fatima had learned an important lesson. "And I thank Allah for giving you a son like him."

"And why would you be so thankful about me having someone like Thomas?"

"Because he is a wonderful child and extremely intelligent. Would you not agree?"

"Yes, he is very intelligent, but how can you know all these things when you've only just met him?"

"Gay people can spot one another miles away," he said beaming. "I know you brought him with you to meet his grandparents, but I also think you want to know as a parent what to do with someone like Thomas. Or am I mistaken?"

"No, you are right just like you were when we first met," she acknowledged. "And I really need some advice, because I want him to know that I love him no matter what he is."

Mustafa leaned forward in his chair as he spoke. "I can tell he already knows you love him, little cousin," he said as if love wasn't the problem. "You did the best thing any parent could do for someone like Thomas. You taught him to know God by showing him how to read the Holy Quran, which was the same thing my stepfather, Ali, did for me! That was a great accomplishment because he knows God is watching everything he does."

Fatima folded her hands on the dining room table like a judge listening to a lawyer's closing arguments.

"All you can do at this point is continue to love him and Allah will do the rest," continued Mustafa. "And let me add this little piece of advice. No one knows what God will do about people like me and Thomas. So, as far as I am concerned, Allah is the only one I am going to worry about!"

Fatima felt as if a great weight had been lifted from her shoulders. "That is exactly what my father said."

Mustafa raised the goblet in the air. "And may Allah continue to guide you and your son, my dear cousin," he said swallowing what remained in the cup.

Mustafa and Fatima were interrupted by the sound of Miriam and Thomas entering the dining hall. "This place is beautiful," exclaimed Thomas. "I can't wait to tell Dad about everything."

"Your father has already been here, Emilio, although that was a long time ago."

"How come I'm always the last one to find out everything?"

"Do not worry, little cousin. A day will come when being first to know something can be worse than finding out later," warned Mustafa.

The dining room door suddenly burst opened. "MIRIAM

COME QUICKLY, OMAR IS NOT BREATHING!" screamed Aisha standing at the doorway.

Miriam and everyone else at the table bolted out of the hall and in the direction of Aisha's bedroom. Miriam was the first to arrive at Omar's bedside, followed by Aisha and Fatima. Mustafa stood at the doorway holding Thomas by the shoulders to prevent him from seeing his grandfather's body. Omar's face was pale and lifeless. His eyes were open. There was an expression of contentment on his facial features. Miriam used her fingers to close Omar's eyes. Aisha fell on top of her husband's body. She laid her head on his chest while sobbing at the loss of someone she had been married to for almost a half century. Fatima sat on the edge of the bed and placed one hand on her mother's shoulder.

FORTY EIGHT

I BECAME a third-degree black belt, three years after enrolling at the karate school and the only one that wore tennis shoes when competing against an opponent. Mister Toomey also reminded me not to pick fights, like William McDuffie did with Freddy, because I had the ability injure someone permanently. My dad was very surprised when he found out I intended to take up karate. He thought I disliked things requiring a lot of physical contact. It's true, I was afraid of getting into fights because I had never learned to defend myself, but after becoming a black belt everything about me changed. Even my personality. To say that I owe everything to Frederick Steinberg would be an understatement. Freddy not only encouraged me to take up karate, but he also gave me an understanding about God quite different from the way my mother did, and I will always be indebted to him because he made me realize I was no different than anyone else.

My dad wasn't only surprised about me learning to protect myself, he decided one Saturday morning in the summer of 1957 to see if I was still this insecure person he was trying to raise as a father. He was at the kitchen table eating breakfast. I walked into the kitchen wearing my karate suit and tennis shoes and wanted to eat something before Freddy came to take me to the karate school. Freddy spent a lot of his weekends going out with Katheryn Cross, who still worked part-time at the school and attended Fashion Industries High School full-time. They had been going steady for the last three years and planned to get married after all of us graduated. After Freddy told Katheryn the reason why he smacked her brother that day in school, she didn't seem upset. But that's another story.

"Morning, Dad," I said smiling.

"Morning, Thomas. Where are you going so early in the morning?

"To my karate class with Freddy." I said opening the refrigerator and taking out a container of milk.

"Does he take lessons with you?"

"No, he goes with me to see his girlfriend who works there as a secretary," I said putting the milk on the table. "And anyway, Freddy is Captain of the Weightlifting Team at Dartmouth High, so he doesn't have to learn how to fight."

My dad was wearing pajamas, house slippers, and a bathrobe. My mom was upstairs sleeping.

"When are you going to be a first-degree black belt like the Japanese people are?"

I took a box of Wheaties, along with a large bowl, from out of the cupboard and placed everything beside the milk. "I'm already a third degree right now," I said filling the bowl with cereal and pouring milk on top, "but it's going to take a little while longer before I reach the first-degree level."

"I've always wanted to learn karate and I'm really happy you're learning to protect yourself," he said raising a cup of coffee to his lips.

"So am I," I said sitting down and bowing my head to say grace over my food.

My dad waited until I finished saying grace before he spoke. "What's the difference between a black-belt and a brown belt?" he asked, putting the cup on the saucer.

"Experience. The more fights you win, the higher your rating gets."

"How many fights have you had?"

"I don't know, maybe two hundred or more," I said putting a spoon full of cereal into my mouth.

"Really, that many huh?"

"Yeah, but they weren't easy. I had to develop my own style, so my opponent couldn't figure me out. It's a little hard to explain, but it has a lot to do with the way I start out which helps me to win."

"You don't say. Why don't you show me what you mean?"

I didn't know if my dad wanted to see some of my techniques or was trying to find out if I was really a black belt, so I made up my mind to show him some footwork which helped me become an expert. As soon as we finished eating, we went to the patio in front of the house. The weather was hot. I kept my jacket on because I just wanted to show him some different positions many professionals use. Nevertheless, my dad didn't want to see any footwork. He just wanted to see how I would defend myself if somebody tried to attack me. He took a stack of newspapers from off the patio table, rolled them up like a "Billy Club" and walked towards me.

"Don't you want to see some of the footwork I use?" I said, hoping he didn't want to fight.

"No, no, no, I don't want you to show me anything," he insisted. "I just want to see if you know your stuff."

My dad started hitting me across the shoulder with the Billy Club. I backed up, not wanting to punch or kick him.

"Hey, I thought you said you were a black-belt, or are you just one of those sissies who likes to wear a karate suit?"

I stared at my dad, wondering if he really meant what he said about me being a sissy. I decided to walk away because I was really offended by his remark.

"Hey, Mr. Black-belt, where are you going?" he said, grabbing my arm. "I thought you was going to show me some of your tricks, mister chicken."

My dad started hitting me over the head with the newspapers. I decided to teach him a lesson about calling me a sissy and grabbed his wrist with my left hand. He tried to break free. I hit him in the middle of his forehead with the heel of my right hand, causing his head to snap backwards. He also began staggering away from me and towards the patio table. I was going to punch him in the throat with my fist, while holding his wrist, but I knew it would put him in the hospital. I turned sideways and kicked him between the legs like a football player kicking a field goal. The fact that I was wearing tennis shoes helped ease the pain that he would have felt if I had used my bare foot. He immediately dropped the Billy Club and grabbed my shoulders with both hands to keep from falling. I knew he was in tremendous pain and allowed him to hold on to my shoulders for support as we knelt very slowly on the patio floor together. I tried to help him stand up, but he began to groan from the pain he was feeling after being kicked between the legs. I decided to stand up and leave him on his knees holding his crotch with both hands.

"I guess I had that coming?" he said with his face distorted.

"Yeah, you did," I said unsympathetically.

"Hey, little brother, are you ready?" said a voice behind me.

I turned around. Freddy was walking towards my house with car keys in his hand and wearing a grey sweat suit and white tennis shoes. I began walking to the convertible Freddy was driving.

"What's your father doing on his knees?" Freddy asked, staring at the man wearing a bathrobe.

"He called me a sissy, so I kicked him in the balls!" I said walking passed Freddy.

"You did what?" Freddy said walking behind me.

I turned around. "I'm never going to let anybody call me a sissy again, including my father!" I said angrily.

Freddy started laughing. "So, you decided to kick him in the balls?"

"Yeah, he had it coming," I said walking to the car.

FORTY NINE

THE TIME WAS 2:26 P.M. The Sergeant was sitting on the couch with his arms over the backseat. "What time did you tell Phillip to be here with David?" he inquired.

"Four o'clock sharp," she said perched on the couch beside him. "What do you think will happen if we prove David is guilty of murder?"

"He'll go to prison, and I hope for the rest of his life," he said bluntly. "He's just lucky I didn't find out what really happened, or he would be in his goddamn grave right now!"

"So, you want me to make both of them believe I'm really not dead, even though I look like my mother?"

The Sergeant chuckled. "That's the plan, since all you've got is your word against his," he said straightforwardly. "Just make David believe you're Thomas and willing to work things out if he comes clean. But also say your father doesn't care about a confession and wants David to go to the gas chamber."

"David will never go for that good cop bad cop routine, he's too smart for that."

"Oh yes he will after you tell him what really happened and that you weren't standing by the door like his report says."

"I wish I had those pictures I took of him, then it wouldn't matter if he believed me or not."

Someone knocked on the office door. "Come in," said Rosemary.

The secretary opened the door. "A young lady named Katheryn Cross is here to see you, Your Honor," she said courteously.

"Send her in," said Rosemary surprised.

The secretary stepped aside and allowed an attractive girl of twenty- three to enter the chambers. She had on a loose-fitting dress worn by pregnant women and a shoe box under her arm. The secretary closed the door.

"Hello, Mrs. Shumsky," she said looking at Rosemary. "My name is Katheryn. We've never met, but I know your son because he used to go to the karate school where I work."

"You must be Frederick Steinberg's girlfriend?" said Rosemary rising to her feet. "My son used to talk a lot about you and Frederick. This is my husband, Mr. Shumsky"

"How do you do, Mr. Shumsky?"

"The pleasure's all mine, Katheryn."

"Why don't you have a seat beside my husband?"

Katheryn sat on the couch with the shoebox on her lap. Rosemary remained standing.

"What brings you to my office?"

"Frederick gave me this shoe box to give to his father, but I thought you should have it instead," she said giving the shoebox to Rosemary and sitting down again. "It has the pictures your son took of my brother getting money from the immigrants my father was blackmailing."

Rosemary glanced at the Sergeant as she walked to the couch with the shoebox under her arm. "This is going to be very helpful," she said sitting beside Katheryn, "but may I ask you a personal question?"

"Yes ma'am."

"Why would you give me these photographs, knowing David and your father could lose their jobs, as well as get arrested?" she said putting the shoebox on her lap.

"Because my fiancé lost his job and his life!" she charged. "When Frederick told me about them being dishonest, I didn't want to believe it was true. But After David killed Frederick, I knew everything Frederick said was the truth."

"So, you don't believe Frederick's death was an accident?" uttered the Sergeant.

"No, David hated Frederick ever since they were in high school together, so I know it wasn't accidental. Don't get me wrong, Mr. Shumsky, I love my family, but I loved Frederick too, because he cared about me as a person and not because I was attractive."

Katheryn rose from the couch. The Sergeant quickly stood up and shook hands with Katheryn. "Thank you, Miss Cross, for giving my son those pictures," he said gratefully.

"Your son?" said Katheryn puzzled.

"I meant, my wife," he frowned looking dumbfounded.

"I'm going to call my first baby, Thomas, after your son," said Katheryn looking at Rosemary. "And if it's a girl, I'll call her…"

"Thomasina," said Rosemary finishing the sentence.

"Yes, how did you know?"

"My son told me Freddy made him that promise before they were killed. I want you to stay in touch, so me and my husband can be the baby's godparents."

"I will," said Katheryn walking to the door. "Goodbye, Mrs. Shumsky."

"Goodbye, Katheryn."

"Goodbye, Mr. Shumsky."

"Goodbye, Katheryn, and thanks for everything," said the Sergeant waving his hand.

FIFTY

OMAR'S FUNERAL was held at Miriam Akbar's Estate. After the ceremony, she arranged for his body to be taken to the Town of Ta'if and buried alongside his ancestors. Aisha accompanied her husband's casket back to Ta'if and then returned to Antioch to spend the remaining days of her life at Miriam's home with her nephew, Mustafa. Fatima decided not to go to Ta'if because the journey would be time consuming and wanted to return to New York City before her husband became aware she and Emilio were gone. However, Fatima had difficulty getting out of the country because the picture on her passport matched the photograph of a woman wanted by the Arab Government in connection with the murder of two soldiers near a church in Antioch 14 years ago! Fatima called Phillip Cross and told him about not being the real Rosemary Shumsky and wanted by the Ottoman Empire for murdering the soldiers. Phillip had helped Fatima when she needed a birth certificate in the name of Kissinger and decided to assist her once again. Phillip wasn't only the Director of the Immigration Department, he was an Alderman for the Borough of Manhattan, and rather than risk the chance of getting caught with assisting a fugitive from justice, he told his son to handle the situation, since they were both in the business of smuggling foreigners into the country anyway. Phillip mentioned to David about the fictitious name she used to come into the United States twelve years ago and that her real name was Fatima Muttalib. David Cross was now a detective in the police department. He started helping his father blackmail immigrants when he first arrived at the 27th precinct and supplied Fatima with a passport in the name of his own mother, Mrs. Ellen Cross. After being told by his father that Fatima and Robert were wanted for murder, David elected not to expose their little secret because the sergeant had just received a Declaration for Bravery from the Mayor of New York for capturing two would-be bank robbers and wounded in the process.

FIFTY ONE

AFTER RETURNING FROM ANTIOCH with Emilio back to America, Fatima decided to try and make her marriage work again. The trip to Miriam Akbar's estate brought back memories of when she and Robert first met and the impression he made on her and the family. She still cared about her husband and knew trying to start over again wasn't going to be easy. Robert had not only been difficult to live with after they were married, but he was also now engulfed with all the publicity he received after coming out of the hospital and being interviewed by dozens of news reporters about capturing the assailants and being injured in the process. Nevertheless, she was willing to forget about the past and try to make a fresh start.

Unfortunately, Robert Shumsky had different thoughts about their marriage and believed it was as good as it was going to get. They both had successful careers and were the envy of everyone who thought they were the perfect couple. And so, Robert Shumsky couldn't be more pleased with himself. After leaving the hospital, he was promoted to lieutenant and enjoyed national attention for heroism. Newspaper and magazine articles, television appearances, and public speaking engagements quickly made him very famous across the country. Movie producers tried seducing him into the world of film making, but he declined the invitation because of his allegiance to the police department. As a result of being in the spotlight for the first time in his career, Robert Shumsky paid no attention to his wife's suggestions that they spend more time together and perhaps renew their wedding vows.

Rosemary quickly realized her husband was not about to change for the sake of their marriage and decided to continue pursuing her own career and become the superior court judge she always wanted to be. And so, her affair with Phillip Cross began. Rosemary concluded it was in her best interest to seduce an influential person like Mr. Cross because of his political connections with the City Officials of New York and use him to become appointed by the Judicial Counsel to be in Municipal Court, which was one step away from becoming a Superior Court Judge. As expected, Phillip Cross became entangled in Fatima's spider web of affairs like everyone else who thought she was one of the most attractive and ambitious district attorneys the criminal justice system had seen in a long time.

FIFTY TWO

WITHOUT WARNING, the pendulum of good fortune for Robert Shumsky began swinging in the opposite direction. Thomas Emilio Shumsky graduated from the academy and came to work at the 27th Precinct with his father in 1962. After becoming a policeman as he his father had hoped, Thomas also became an embarrassment to the family's good name. Everyone at the 27th Precinct knew Thomas Emilio Shumsky was gay, thanks to David Cross spreading rumors about him and saying gay boys don't make good cops. Thomas didn't mind the gossipmongers because of his confidence as a karate expert, but his father didn't feel the same way and began threatening co-workers under his command not to make fun of his son, or else suffer the consequences of dealing with him personally.

Lieutenant Shumsky went all out to protect his son's reputation. After reprimanding everyone, he began physically assaulting those who ignored his warning. David Cross happened to be one of the people the lieutenant put in the hospital with a broken jaw. He was immediately demoted to the rank of sergeant after the Internal Investigation Unit found him guilty of assault and battery on a fellow employee. The only reason criminal charges weren't filed was due to his outstanding achievements as a policeman and heroic acts of courage when faced with life threatening situations. Robert didn't mind being reduced to sergeant. Jewish blood was thicker than administrative water and protecting his son's image came first, regardless of the consequences. However, David Cross never forgot about the broken jaw he received, as well as the fact that the investigation concerning the assault on him was all a sham, and swore he would get even someday, somewhere, and somehow.

The following month, Robert Shumsky's career took another turn for the worse. He was assigned to the precinct as desk sergeant. Phillip Cross, who was still Alderman for the City, didn't take too kindly to his son being hospitalized and made sure Sergeant Shumsky was relegated to the position of an office clerk, since the department wouldn't retire him.

FIFTY THREE

WITH NOTHING but a desk job to look forward to everyday, Robert Bernard Shumsky knew he wasn't the same person who had been awarded a medal for bravery, and began contemplating the idea of leaving the department, even though he needed a few more years to retire with a pension. In addition to everything else, his marriage turned out to be a complete disaster because of his inability to carry out the responsibilities of marriage, which included that he is not a domineering husband and prevent his wife from being the kind of mother that Thomas Emilio Shumsky needed as he was growing up. Last, but not least, Robert's inability to accept his son as he was, had bothered him ever since he put David Cross in the hospital with a broken jaw.

Believing his marriage to Fatima was beyond repair, Robert intended to give her a divorce at the end of the year, leave the 27th Precinct without receiving a full pension, and let his son do whatever he needed to do to fix his own problem. But just when he thought things couldn't get any worst, Thomas Emilio Shumsky was shot in his own apartment by Detective David Cross and died at the scene. Newspapers quickly circulated stories about the Shumsky Family having a legacy of heroes in their bloodline and Thomas Shumsky's death was connected to an unquestionable act of courage and in the line of duty.

FIFTY FOUR

ROSEMARY SHUMSKY was presiding over a jury trial when she received the news about her son being shot in his apartment by Detective David Cross and Emilio dying at the scene. The time was 8:05 a.m. The date was August 11, 1963. She immediately rushed to the coroner's office to identify Emilio's body and cried for more than an hour before being asked to leave so an autopsy could be performed, which the coroner, James Miller, insisted she shouldn't witness because the examination and inspection of dead bodies were often too gruesome to look at. Mr. Miller gave her the box of civilian clothes Thomas wore when he was shot. Rosemary tried contacting her husband, even though they had been separated for several weeks, but Robert had taken the afternoon off from his desk job and was expected to return the following day. Rosemary and Robert had been separated for the last few weeks because Robert had become difficult to live with after being demoted from lieutenant to sergeant and assigned a desk job. Rosemary took her son's clothes to the courthouse because she had left some personal belongings at the office. She put the box of civilian clothes on the couch, grabbed her purse, and went home. She was still unable to get in contact with Robert the entire evening and believed he was doing his own investigation concerning their son's death. The following morning, she returned to the courthouse and sent word to the 27th Precinct for David Cross to come to her office immediately. She also had the jury trial she was presiding over transferred to Judge Raymond's Courtroom, although she didn't want to do it. The case in volved an officer shooting an unarmed civilian and Raymond's policy was policemen were always right, so there was a good chance he would make sure the officer's actions were vindicated.

Rosemary walked to the couch, opened the box, and thought about today being August 12, 1963. This was the day she and Emilio were supposed to go out together and have dinner in celebration of being born in the same month and on the same day. She took out his grey sweatshirt. There was blood on the front of the shirt as well as on the sleeves. Rosemary kept staring at the sleeves. The coroner said Emilio had been shot in the abdomen. Why was there blood on the sleeve, she asked herself ? Rosemary lifted the shirt to her nose. The scent of Emilio's body odor was still under the arm pits. She put the shirt down and pulled out the pair of old dingy white tennis shoes he wore when he was shot by David Cross. Rosemary's eyes became watery as she looked at the gold framed picture on her desk of Emilio dressed in his karate suit and the shoes she was holding in her hand. Emilio gave her the photograph to keep after becoming a black belt in martial arts.

"Why do you wear shoes, Emilio?" she remembered asking him the day he brought the picture to her office. "I thought you couldn't wear shoes?"

Emilio said people don't usually wear shoes when they're competing against one another, but he wanted to be different. He also said they were his lucky shoes and made him feel like Allah was always watching over him whenever he put them on. Now Emilio was dead. Shot by Detective David Cross in the same shoes he believed had some type of spiritual connection with God. Whatever divine relationship Emilio thought they had with protecting him from some type of misfortune, it did not save him from being slain by another policeman, she thought. Rosemary decided to keep the shoes someplace in her office because it would always remind her of Emilio being a karate expert. She looked around the chambers for a place to hang the shoes. She noticed his picture had been framed in gold and decided to have the shoes gold plated. The cost would be expensive, but sentiments such as this one do not carry a price tag, she reminded herself.

Rosemary put on the shoes to get an idea of how she wanted them to be gold plated. As soon as she tied the laces on both shoes, she immediately lost consciousness and fell to the floor. A few seconds later, she opened her eyes, stood up from the floor, and began inspecting the room. Something was wrong. "How did I get into my mother's office, when I was in my apartment just a few minutes ago?" Thomas Emilio Shumsky asked himself!

Thomas looked at his feet. He was still wearing his tennis shoes, but when he looked at the back of his hands, he noticed his fingernails were polished with red enamel. After looking at the sleeves of his clothes, he immediately realized he was dressed in the same black robe his mother wears when sitting on the bench. He placed his hands over his chest. Thomas Emilio Shumsky suddenly became aware that he was now a woman, and it wasn't until he glanced at the wedding picture of his parents on top of the desk that it dawned on him, he was also Rosemary Patricia Shumsky, his own mother!

"This can't be happening," he said to himself, while surveying the chambers for some rational explanation about his reincarnation.

He remembered arguing with David Cross about Frederick Steinberg, because Freddy had been shot by David and was still alive. The last thing he remembered was walking towards the bedroom to use the telephone to call an ambulance and take Freddy to the hospital. Thomas Shumsky was confounded.

"This was impossible," he kept saying over and over. How could he come back from the dead as a woman? And worst of all, his own mother. Thomas ran to the desk, picked up the phone, and called the 27th Precinct hoping to talk with his father.

"Sergeant's desk, Officer Clark speaking," said the voice on the other end.

"Is Sergeant Shumsky there?" said Thomas frantically.

"No, he isn't," replied the voice. "He stepped away from his desk for a moment. May I help you?"

"Tell him his wife, Judge Rosemary Shumsky, wants to see him right away and that it's urgent."

"Yes ma'am, I'll tell him right now," responded the voice.

Thomas Emilio Shumsky hung up the phone and commenced to pace the floor of his mother's chambers in a pair of tennis shoes, wondering how he was going to convince his dad he was alive again.

FIFTY FIVE

AS SOON AS ME AND FREDDY graduated from Dartmouth High School in 1957, I took Freddy's advice and decided to try and be this so-called honest cop he claimed I was capable of becoming. My father was happy. My mother wasn't so thrilled. She didn't think I was cut out to be a policeman and should've been a photographer. I had to wait for four years before I could go to the academy, which didn't bother me because I used the time to perfect my karate skills in many of the tournaments I competed in.

I had two problems after enrolling at the academy. Everyone expected me to be the top student in my class because my father and grandfather graduated with flying colors. Unfortunately, that didn't happen. I had difficulty making quick decisions when it affected me and another police officer working together during a tactical maneuver. The second problem was shooting guns. Being a black belt made it hard to think about using firearms when I knew a few kicks and punches were safer than bullets. Nevertheless, Frederick Steinberg helped me to overcome my reluctance to use weapons with private lessons in using pistols at the gun club where his father and Rabbi Jacob were members. I learned to be a sharpshooter very quickly and intended to use that skill just to wound someone rather than kill them. Finally, at age twenty-two, I completed my training and became a cop in 1962. What I didn't know until I started working at the twenty seventh precinct was that David Cross had been a policeman at the same station since 1959 and was now a detective in the fraud division. After finding out I was working there, David began spreading rumors about me being gay, which quickly put a blemish on my family's good name. My dad, who was lieutenant and commander over the robbery and fraud division, did everything possible to stop everyone under his command from trying to embarrass me. But the more he demanded they respect me, the more they disregarded his orders. During my first year in the force, my dad had a run in with David Cross and put him in the hospital with a broken jaw for drawing a cartoon of me being screwed in the butt by someone I had arrested. After a long and lengthy investigation by the Internal Affairs Committee, my dad was demoted to sergeant and given a desk job because the committee found him guilty of using excessive force on a fellow employee.

I wasn't really bothered by what my co-workers said about me. Being a karate expert taught me a lot about humility and how to ignore people who enjoyed ridiculing others. As a third-degree black belt, I outgrew a lot of insecurities I had in high school and was asked to put on a few karate exhibitions with other martial arts experts at the Police Academy. Those demonstrations made it clear to a lot of people who had mixed feelings about me, what the difference was between a gay person and someone who knew how to kick-ass and take names! And no one at the Twenty Seventh Precinct ever made fun of me to my face, since my reputation as an expert in karate preceded me.

FIFTY SIX

WORKING AT THE TWENTY SEVENTH STATION gave me an opportunity to see how Negro people lived in Harlem New York. I was assigned to patrol the metropolitan area where clothing stores, night clubs, and a lot of movie theaters were located. The people had a lifestyle very different from any culture I knew about. While on patrol in the summer, I became accustomed to seeing men in front of tenement buildings shooting dice in public without fear of being arrested. I also saw prostitutes on the corner of Eighth Avenue, unafraid of being seen by patrol cars like mine. I learned as a rookie the twenty seventh station had a hands-off policy for the community, just so long as they didn't go outside the radius of Harlem when committing small infractions like gambling and solicitation. Most of my time during the month of August in 1962 was spent issuing out parking tickets to pimps and drug dealers who left their expensive automobiles sitting in front of fire hydrants or inside a no parking zone. I also gave out summons to people that left their vehicles double parked and unattended while they congregated inside local bars like Club Fantasy. The Club Fantasy was a well-known bar and lounge where mostly gay people socialized and was located on one hundred and twenty fifth street, between Saint Nicholas and Eighth Avenue. It was owned by a transvestite from South America named Chi Chi Quintana. I didn't find out Chi Chi was a transvestite until after I went to a birthday party she gave at the club she owned and told by someone at the party who knew her. The first time I met Chi Chi was on her birthday. She came running out of her establishment and began yelling at me about her four- door sedan being hitched up to a tow truck because it had caused a huge traffic jam.

"Where are you taking my car?" she said angrily.

"To the impound on fifty fifth street," I said politely. "You can go there, pay the fine, and get it back tonight. But it has to go because it was in a no parking zone and that's a serious violation."

I gave Chi Chi the parking ticket as she stood in front of me wearing a blond wig and full-length dress. She was very attractive and looked like a real woman. Chi Chi stared at me and smiled. Something about her expression told me she knew we had something in common as gay people. "What's your sign, Mr. Shumsky?" she said looking at the name plate over my shirt pocket.

"I'm a Leo."

"Are you married?" she asked, fanning herself from the heat with the parking ticket.

"Why all the questions?" I said putting a small black book with blank parking tickets into my back pocket.

"Because I'm a Leo myself and would like for you to come with some of my other policemen friends to a birthday party I'm having tonight in my club."

"What other policemen friends?"

"Do you know Detective Cross?"

"You mean, David Cross?"

"Yes," she smiled. "I invited him and his father to my party."

"His father works for the Department of Immigration, so why is he coming?"

"Him and David helped me, and my family come to America from Cuba many years ago and I always invite them to my parties."

I wondered if Phillip Cross and his son were in the business of smuggling foreigners into the country illegally. I remember when me and my mother were in Antioch visiting my grandparents and she had to call Phillip because something was wrong with her passport. Mr. Cross was able to get us back home the same day, although I think she had to pay him some money for doing us a big favor.

"So, will you be here tonight?" she said continuing to fan herself.

"I might stop by if I'm in the neighborhood," I replied, wondering what to wear at a gay party in Harlem.

"Good, I'll see you this evening," she said happily. "And you can tell them at the door I said you're a guest and don't have to pay to get in."

Chi Chi Quintana walked away and waved at a taxicab to take her to the impound on fifty fifth street.

FIFTY SEVEN

THE MUSIC WAS LOUD. The club Fantasy was filled with gay boys, drag queens, lesbians, and dykes dressed in expensive clothing and dancing with each other. Those who weren't dancing were sitting on stools at the bar drinking all kinds of alcoholic beverages and chatting with each other, while the other people socialized at tables around the room. I was wearing a blue short-sleeved shirt and a pair of dungaree pants. I also had the tennis shoes I like to wear when competing in karate matches. I wanted to try and look inconspicuous, so I wouldn't bring a lot of attention on myself but forgot that being a white boy at a night club in Harlem would make me stand out like a sore thumb. No sooner was I inside, did everyone begin staring at me as if I was wearing my policemen's uniform. I ignored the stares and strolled over to the bar to order a drink. Every seat was occupied. I stood behind someone I thought was a female. She wore a short skirt, high heel shoes, and weighed about a hundred and fifty pounds.

"Excuse me, but would you order me a drink from the bar please?" I said politely.

The female turned around on her stool. I suddenly realized he was a drag queen because the makeup on his face couldn't hide the shadow from using razor blades. Not to mention the "Adam's Apple" sticking out from his throat. There was an empty bottle of champagne, and a glass half filled with alcohol in front of the drag queen.

"What are you drinking?" he said femininely.

I put both hands into my pants pockets. "Some milk," I said politely.

"Milk!?" he said surprised. "Listen honeybunch, you've come to the wrong place just to order some milk. This ain't a restaurant, it's a nightclub in case you haven't noticed. And a glass of milk costs as much as a drink, so you might as well order scotch and milk."

Something about the way the drag queen talked made me start laughing. "What are you drinking?" I asked.

"I'm drinking a split darling, and it cost seven dollars a holler."

"Tell the bartender to give you another split and a glass of milk on the side," I said as though money were no object. "That way I can have the milk, and you can have the split."

"Well, all right big spender" he said snapping his finger in the air.

The drag queen turned back around to face the bottles of liquor on the shelves in front of us.

"Lucille, give me another split and a glass of Vitamin D. for Mr. Rockefeller over here."

I started laughing again. The drag queen ordering the split and glass of milk wasn't attractive, but he had a nice figure and lively personality, which made up for what he lacked in good looks. "My name's Trixie," he said turning around to face me again. "Some people think it's my profession, but it's just a stage name, not what I do for a living."

Trixie held out his hand for me to shake.

"My name's Thomas Shumsky," I said shaking hands.

"You've got quite a grip, Mr. Shumsky," he said flexing his fingers after we shook hands. "It's been said people with firm handshakes are very confident about themselves. Wouldn't you agree?"

"I don't know about that," I replied modestly, "but there was a time when I wasn't so self- assured as I am now. So, I guess I owe a lot of my confidence to karate lessons."

"Are you a karate expert?"

"I'm a black belt, but not a first degree yet."

"Really," he said impressed. "Are you a bodyguard or something?"

"No, karate is just a hobby. I'm really a police officer."

"Well, aren't you full of surprises?" he said, crossing his legs.

"Here you go, Trixie," said the skinny barmaid with long black hair, placing the glass of milk and small bottle of champagne on the counter in front of us. "That'll be seven dollars for the split and one fifty for the milk."

I gave the barmaid twelve dollars. "Keep the change," I said picking up the milk and taking a sip.

"Thank you," said the barmaid as she walked away.

"And where have you been all my life?" Trixie said after seeing me give Lucille a large tip.

I almost choked on the milk as I laughed again.

"Would you mind if I asked you a personal question?" Trixie said unscrewing the cap on the bottle and pouring a drink.

"Sure, go ahead."

"Do you have anything to do with the Immigration Department?"

"Why do you ask?"

"Because Miss Quintana seems to have a lot of friends who are cops and all they do is take advantage of people from other countries like my friend, Muhammad."

"You mean the same lady that invited me to this party?"

"Yes, but she's no lady. She's a transvestite," Trixie said in a voice that was envious.

"You sound as if you don't really like Miss Quintana."

"Actually, I do like her, but she can be a real bitch sometimes because she doesn't want people like me use the lady's room instead of the men's room, when we have to use the toilet."

I began smiling as though I understood from Trixie's point of view that being a drag queen also meant acting out the part in public. "What did you mean when you said, Miss Quintana's friends take advantage of people?"

"Miss Quintana has a friend who is a cop, and he charges people a lot of money to get them and their families into New York City."

Trixie drank the champagne from his glass until it was empty.

"Don't get me wrong, living here is better than a lot of those other countries you read about," he continued, "but this cop doesn't really make you a legal citizen. All he does is threaten to send you back to your own country if you don't keep paying him every month."

"So, as long as you stay here, you have to pay or be deported?"

"Yeah, and he gets two hundred bucks a month from each family. Which comes to a lot of doe when you count over twenty or thirty families."

Trixie turned around, grabbed the champagne bottle from off the counter, and drank the alcohol straight out of the bottle.

"How did you find all this out?" I said believing it was true.

"Because my friend pays this cop," he said slamming the empty bottle on the counter and facing me again. "And I think it's wrong, since he's a poor man and can hardly support his family."

"What kind of work does your friend do?"

"He drives a cab like me. That's how we met. I picked him and his family up from the airport. He was born in Antioch and worked for some rich broad who gave him the money to come to the states. He just didn't think he was going to keep paying once he got here."

I wondered if Miriam Akbar was the rich lady Trixie was talking about. I drank the rest of my milk and put the glass on the counter.

"I wish there were some honest cops around this goddamn

place, so those fucking white cops like Chi Chi's friends could go to jail for taking advantage of people like Muhammad," said Trixie disgusted.

I thought about what Frederick Steinberg said in the restaurant when we first met five years ago. "New York needs a lot of good cops, not just a few." Part of me wished I could help people like Trixie's friend, but I knew it would take more than just myself to stop Phillip Cross, who had been working for the Immigration's department over forty years and probably behind the whole scam.

"Excuse me while I use the men's room," I said patting Trixie on the shoulder as if I understood his concern about Muhammad.

FIFTY EIGHT

I WALKED OUT OF THE MEN'S ROOM and came face to face with Chi Chi Quintana. She looked like a model on the cover of a Cosmopolitan Magazine, with long blond hair, false eye lashes, and a face smeared with makeup. She wore a sleeveless satin dress designed to show off her large breasts and a diamond necklace above the cleavage. Long gemstones dangled from both ears. On her feet were silver satin shoes to match the evening gown. Chi Chi was holding a half-filled glass of champagne as she spoke. "Where have you been all night with your cute self ?" she said with bloodshot eyes.

"I've been here for a while and was drinking at the bar."

"You look like an undercover cop," she said disapprovingly.

"I didn't know what else to wear."

Chi Chi smiled. "That's all right darling, you look just fine," she said swallowing the other half of alcohol. "I told David and Phillip you were coming, and David said you wouldn't show up because you were too high class for this place. So, I bet him a hundred pesos you would. They're in my V.I.P. Room with Ricky and Jasmine waiting to see if you'll show up. Come on let's go."

Me and Chi Chi strolled arm in arm to the rear of the nightclub. I could smell incense burning in the hallway leading to the V.I.P Room. Chi Chi opened the door. The fluorescent light bulbs on the ceiling in the room were dim and the stench of marijuana hit me in the face as I walked through the door. It dawned on me that the coconut incense in the hallway was used to conceal the odor of marijuana in the room. The room was about the size of my mother's office at the courthouse. There was an exit sign above another door on the right side of the compartment. The air conditioner over the exit sign gave the place a comfortable temperature inside.

A handsome light skinned gay boy sat on a couch. The couch was against the wall by the door underneath the exit sign. He was about my age, but much taller, and was sitting beside Phillip Cross. The young man didn't have any clothes on and wore a pair of brief undershorts. Phillip Cross was dressed in a sports jacket, blue jeans, and penny loafers. He sat with his legs crossed and his right arm around the young boy's shoulder.

Sitting a few inches away from Phillip was a white female about twenty-five. She had long dark hair, enormous breasts that were at least a size D-cup, and a black negligee. She looked very sexy. I wasn't sure if she was a real woman or not, but I figured she wasn't because of Chi Chi being a transvestite. David Cross sat next to the female in the negligee. He wore a grey suit, white shirt, and no tie. In front of the couch was a coffee table made of wood. On the table were two bottles of bourbon, four glasses containing liquor and ice, and a large ashtray with half smoked marijuana sticks rolled in white paper. One bottle of bourbon was empty. The other bottle was almost full.

"Well, here he is, smarty pants," bragged Chi Chi, strutting towards David with her hand out. "I told you he would show up. You owe me a hundred pesos, Cabron."

David took a wallet from inside his jacket pocket and gave her a crisp one-hundred-dollar bill. "What brings you to this neck of the woods, Mr. Shumsky?" he said putting the wallet back into his pocket.

Something told me David and his father knew I had come just to see if they would be at the party. "I was about to ask you the same thing," I said nonchalantly.

David grinned as if he knew my attempt to appear sincere was all fake. "My father and I have been coming to Chi Chi's parties ever since she came from Cuba five years ago," he said straightforwardly. "How is it you know Miss Quintana?"

"I gave her a parking ticket today because her car was in no parking zone and holding up traffic."

"And he was so nice about it too," Chi Chi said sticking the hundred- dollar bill into her brassiere.

Phillip Cross removed his arm from around the gay boys shoulder, poured some bourbon into a glass, and leaned back against the sofa. "Would you care for a drink, Thomas?" he said putting his arm around the gay-boy's shoulder again.

Even though Phillip Cross was just putting a show for me in front of everyone, I still appreciated the professional way he acted. "No thanks," I said gratefully. "I've got to get up early for my karate class tomorrow."

"Oh yes, I heard you were some sort of black belt and put on a few exhibitions while training at the academy," Phillip said as he took a sip of bourbon. "I know your mother is very proud of what you've accomplished."

"Yes, she is," I answered happily.

The gay boy folded his arms together and frowned. "Why do you like to take karate classes? That is so macho," he said with a Spanish accent.

I decided not to answer his question, since it was obvious he was confused about someone like me learning to protect himself.

The female sitting next to David Cross also had an accent and sounded like she was from Germany. "Learning to fight is not macho, Ricky, it is being smart," she said smiling at me. "My name is Jasmine Boris."

I wondered for a moment if Jasmine and Ricky were immigrants and had paid their way to come to America. "Nice to meet you, Jasmine," I said nodding.

"Forgive me Thomas, for not introducing you to everyone," Chi Chi said apologizing, "but I was so glad you came I forgot all about it. This is Jasmine Boris and Ricky Munoz."

We all smiled at each other.

Someone began banging on the door like policemen with a search warrant. Everyone stared at Chi Chi as she walked to the door. "Stop banging on my damn door," she said snatching the door open.

Lucille, the skinny barmaid, started talking like she was terrified. "Your bodyguard and Trixie are fighting because Trixie don't wanna use the men's room and Clarence won't let her use the lady's room," Lucille said frightfully.

David and his father started laughing as Chi Chi followed the barmaid to the lady's room. I decided to tag along with Miss Quintana and the barmaid. There was a crowd of spectators at the entrance door of the lady's room. Chi Chi's bodyguard was a six-foot three-inch negro and looked like King Kong. He must have weighed over three hundred pounds and wore a suit jacket too small for his broad shoulders and a necktie too skinny for his chest. He held Trixie's arm with his right hand, while his left hand was around Trixie's neck. Trixie looked helpless.

"Take your goddamn hands off of me," Trixie said, while struggling to break free of the bodyguard's grip around his throat.

"What's going on, Clarence?" Chi Chi said rocking back and forth like she was intoxicated.

"This bitch wants to use the lady's room, and I said no because there are real women using the toilet," he said squeezing Trixie's neck.

"Take your hands from around his neck," I said with authority.

Chi Chi glanced at me and then looked at the bodyguard. "Let her go, Clarence," she said noticing the pitiful look on Trixie's face.

"I'm gonna throw this nigger outside and then I'll let him go," he said dragging Trixie through the crowd.

I ran behind Clarence, snatched him by the back of his pants, and stepped down on the Achilles heel of his right foot with all my strength. Clarence quickly released Trixie's arm and throat and tried to turn around to see who was holding his pants. I immediately stepped down on the same heel, just to make sure he wouldn't give me any problems once I let go of his trousers. Clarence dropped to his knees and clutched his right ankle as if he was in serious pain. I released his pants and walked over to Trixie.

"Are you all right?" I asked with my back to Clarence.

Trixie peered over my shoulder and noticed Clarence hobbling towards me with an angry expression. "LOOK OUT, BEHIND YOU!" Trixie yelled.

I turned around as Clarence tried to snatch me by the neck. I blocked his hand, jumped into the air, and roped my legs around his waist. Then I quickly grabbed him by the back of his head with my left hand. Clarence was so surprised to see my legs circling his body that he didn't see my right hand coming. I hit him in the throat three times very rapidly, not wanting to use my fists because blood would have gone down his windpipe and caused him to die from suffocation. Clarence grabbed his neck with both hands and gasped for breath as he fell backwards on the floor with me sitting on his chest. The crowd of people began cheering as if they were happy to see Clarence get beat up. I stood up on my feet. Clarence remained on the floor holding his throat as though there was something stuck in his windpipe. I walked over to Trixie. "Come on let's go," I said slightly out of breath.

"Thanks, Superman," Trixie said pinching my cheek.

Several people started patting me on the back as me and Trixie headed towards the front entrance. I took Trixie home. He didn't live far from the club, so we walked to the Saint Nicholas Projects on one hundred and twenty seventh street. Trixie thanked me again and said if I ever needed a favor, I could count on him. I took the eighth avenue subway to my home in Staten Island. I called Freddy as soon as I got home and told him every thing that happened at the club, including my fight with Chi Chi's bodyguard. Freddy laughed after I told him how I beat up Clarence and agreed to meet me the next day at the Chinese Restaurant across the street from where he lived.

FIFTY NINE

"I AIN'T SURPRISED David and his old man were at the Club Fantasy," Freddy said distastefully. "You remember when Rabbi Jacob said he thought David could be AC and DC? Maybe David got it from his old man."

"What's AC and DC?" I said curiously.

"A person who likes to have sex with men and women."

"So, you're saying that David is AC and DC because his father is that way?"

"You didn't hear that from me, Mr. Shumsky," Freddy said making fun of Rabbi Jacob.

We laughed.

"You remember when the Rabbi told me in the bathroom that Phillip Cross donates money to the school every year?"

"Yeah, I remember."

"I knew then he was a crook, and now you have the chance to prove he's a scumbag," Freddy said biting his fingernails.

"What do you mean, I have a chance to prove he's a scumbag?"

"This is your chance to be a hero like your old man," he said spitting his fingernail on the floor. "Can't you see that God is gonna use you to stop Phillip Cross for good."

"But I don't know anything about stopping Phillip Cross, Freddy. I'm just a rookie with no experience like cops have."

"You don't need experience. All you need is evidence. And after you get it, you just take it to your mother, and she'll know what to do."

"Why can't I just tell my father, since he has experience about this kind of stuff ?"

"Because he can't go undercover like you can. David and his father probably think you know they smuggle people into the country, since Choo Choo Santana introduced you to everyone at the party."

"You mean, Chi Chi Quintana."

"Yeah, Miss Quintana," he said searching for more nails to chew on. "All you gotta do is tell David Cross you need to get some people from Syria into the United States like his father did when he helped your mother."

"But I don't know anybody in Syria."

"Yes, you do," he said quickly. "You know that rich widow named Miriam Makeba, who lives in Bangkok."

"You mean, Miriam Akbar. And she lives in Antioch, not Bangkok," I said shaking my head as if this whole idea was crazy.

"Yeah whatever," he said like names didn't matter. "Listen, little brother, this is your chance to do something great like your old man did when he caught them bank robbers and got shot."

"Well, I sure don't want to get shot trying to catch somebody."

"Nobody is gonna shoot you, this is different."

The waitress walked to the table where me and Freddy were sitting. "How do you do, Mr. Thomas?" she said cheerfully. "What do you wish to order?"

"Hello, Mrs. Chang," I said happily. "I'll have some shrimp fried rice and a small coke."

"And what do you wish to have, Mr. Freddy?"

"You know me, Mrs. Chang. I'll have some Fried chicken with rice and gravy," he said leaning back against his chair.

Mrs. Chang wrote down what we ordered and walked away.

"Don't you ever get tired of eating chicken?" I said, waiting for him to give me a good reason why he liked poultry so much.

Freddy started flapping his arms like chickens do when they get excited. "It's funny you should ask me that question because a lot of people want to know the same thing. And you know what I tell them?"

"No, what do you tell them?"

"I tell them I was born on a farm and slept in the same barn with a rooster named Big Dick Henry. After he showed me how to crow the way he did, I started to like girls the same way he liked female chickens, because they would come running into the barn after he finished crowing."

Freddy waited for me to stop laughing, so I could hear the rest of the story, but it was difficult because he had me going.

"Now I said all that to say this," he continued. "Eating chicken reminds me of old Big Dick. He loves chickens and so do I. And that's what makes us who we are. It just runs in our blood, little brother, it just runs in our blood."

Freddy began crowing like a rooster. Everyone in the restaurant began staring at Freddy. I laughed so hard my stomach started hurting.

"So, what are you gonna do, Mister Thomas Shumsky?" Freddy said with a straight face. "Be a hero, or just another cop looking the other way, while Phillip and his son keep smuggling immigrants into the country illegally?"

"I don't know anything about going undercover and building a case against David and his father," I said firmly.

"That's all right, I'll help you. I know all about catching criminals."

"And where did you learn how to catch criminals?"

"From Jack Webb and watching Dragnet on television," he said smiling. "All we need is the facts, little brother, just the facts."

I looked Freddy in the eye, wondering if he had a plan that made sense. "Okay, Dick Tracey, what do we do?" I said realizing he was serious.

"Now you're talking. First thing you gotta do is move out of your house and get your own pad."

"Why?"

"Because we need complete secrecy to setup a sting operation and if you stay at home someone will catch on."

I wanted to tell Freddy that one wrong move could mean criminal charges pressed against us for a bunch of laws we would be breaking, not to mention the embarrassment I would bring upon myself for doing something with no experience. Nevertheless, Frederick Steinberg was right. I had to do something as a cop, and this might be the only chance I would get to help people like Trixie's friend, Muhammad, and whoever else Phillip Cross had on his list of people being blackmailed.

"I've got a better idea, why don't I just get an apartment without telling my parents. That way my mother won't worry and start coming around to see me every day."

"So, you want to get another pad but still stay with your folks?"

"Yeah."

"Good idea."

SIXTY

IT TOOK ME AND FREDDY SIX MONTHS to put our plan together because I wanted to wait until I received my vacation time from the police department before we got started. I also used a lot of the days given to me for sick leave just so that everything would work out the way we intended. In February of 1963, we started putting this undercover operation into effect. I let Freddy decide where we would set everything up and he found a one-bedroom apartment in a four-story building on Riverside Drive near the Rockefeller Cathedral. There was a view of the Hudson River, which separated Manhattan Island and New Jersey, from the living room window. The apartment was already furnished and consisted of a large bedroom, small living room, kitchenette, and bathroom. Freddy suggested we use the bedroom to put whatever evidence we came across on the wall.

The first thing we did was pay a visit to Trixie's home to find out where his friend, Muhammad, lived. Trixie was very eager to help us after I told him me and Freddy were going undercover to gather evidence against Phillip and his son. Trixie drove us in his cab to Muhammad's home in Brooklyn. As it turned out, Muhammad knew Miriam Akbar and had worked for her before she gave him the money to come to America. He immediately said he would help to build a case against Phillip and the place where he worked keeps records of all immigrants who pay to have their visa cards renewed once a year. Muhammad also said I could find out who the other aliens were because it was public information.

It took four long months to find out who the foreigners were and where they lived and another month to interview them. We pretend to be employees from the Immigration Department and just making sure they weren't having any trouble with their citizenship. We learned that Phillip was collecting money from more than two hundred families for the past twenty-five years and receiving three hundred dollars from each household every six months. More than fifty people were willing to come forward and testify about making payments to Phillip Cross twice a year. However, Freddy had me take pictures of the foreigners giving money to Phillip's son for more evidence, since it was the month of June and time for the first payoffs to be made. Having experience with cameras made it easy to catch David accepting the payments. Trixie drove me around in the cab, so I wouldn't look suspicious while taking pictures. Some photos were of David getting money in an envelope as he sat in an unmarked car. Other images were of him meeting immigrants on street corners, public parks, and sidewalk cafes. At the end of July, I had over a hundred snapshots. Freddy advised me to take pictures of all the information we had pasted on the wall of the bedroom just in case we needed more proof.

On August 11, 1963, and just one day away from me and my mother's birthday, I was ready to take all the evidence we put together over a five-month period to my mother. What me and Freddy didn't know before we started, was there were several different ways immigrants could become legal citizens. All they needed to do was remain in the country for at least five years, which would entitle them to become U.S. Citizens. The truth was they thought it would be a one-time fee to acquire the visa, and after five years be allowed to remain in the country. However, Phillip Cross had them believe differently, since he was the Immigration Department's Manager and kept them under his thumb like a slave master with a cotton plantation.

"I've got some good news and some bad news," Freddy said putting all the negatives from the pictures I took into a shoebox. "Which do you want to hear first?"

"Let me hear the bad news," I said not knowing if he was serious.

"The bad news is Katheryn is pregnant!" he said distressed. "She called me on the phone at my pad and said she was two months."

"So, what's the good news?"

"Wait, I haven't told you all the bad news yet. She doesn't know we're trying to send her father and brother to prison either."

Me and my best friend stared at each other for a long time. Then I gazed around the bedroom at all the pictures taped on the wall, along with the names and addresses of the people we interviewed, not knowing what to say to someone I had grown to love as my own brother. I knew Freddy and Katheryn were very serious about each other because they had been going steady ever since I had that fight with William McDuffie at the karate school.

"What do you think she'll do when you tell her?" I said finally.

"I wish I knew, little brother," he said sadly. "All I thought about when we started this operation was how am I gonna say that her old man is a crook? And now that she's pregnant, I really don't know what to tell her."

"I've been meaning to ask you something about Katheryn, but I just didn't know how to say it," I said hoping Freddy wouldn't be upset.

"What's that?"

"Is Katheryn AC and DC?"

"Naw, she's straight," he said happily. "And I'll tell you something else. I believe she knows her father and brother like to go to swap meets every now and then."

"What makes you say that?"

"Because she didn't seem surprised when I told her what the Rabbi said about her brother trying to seduce his son."

"Wait a minute, you actually told her what the Rabbi said to you in school that day?"

"Yeah, because she wanted to know why I hit her brother, and I told her."

"And you told her about me?"

"Yep, and she knows you're my best friend and that only God has the right to judge gay people," he said putting the top on the shoebox. "She is really one hell of a girl."

"So, what's the good news, now that you've told me all the crazy stuff?"

"She wants to get married, so the family won't be embarrassed about her having a baby out of wedlock."

"That's great," I said cheerfully.

"No, it ain't," he disagreed. "We're supposed to have dinner tonight and I haven't mentioned any of the stuff you and I have been doing undercover."

"Are you going to tell her?"

"Yeah, I guess so," he said tucking the shoebox under his arm.

"Where are you going with the shoebox? That's all the stuff we've put together."

"Yeah, I know, that's why I'm giving it to my old man just in case something happens to the originals."

"Does your dad know about everything?"

"Not everything. I told him about Phillip and David being crooks and what they were doing. I just didn't say we were going undercover to prove it."

"Listen Freddy, no matter how this turns out, I just want to say thank you for making me a good cop."

Freddy grinned and then bit the thumbnail on his left hand, while holding the shoebox under his right arm. "It's been a pleasure, Mr. Shumsky," he said like we were business partners, "and I look forward to us becoming very famous for exposing the biggest government scandal in the history of New York City."

I laughed.

"I'll meet you back here tomorrow morning at six o'clock, so we can take this other stuff off the wall and give it to my mother," I said feeling as if we had accomplished something very special. "Oh yeah, I almost forgot. I want you and Katheryn to be at the birthday party I'm having for me and my mother tomorrow night."

"No problem, we'll be there. I'll see you in the morning right back here at the pad."

Freddy left the apartment. I sat on the bed wondering how things were going to play out with Katheryn and Freddy. They had a very special relationship because of her being Caucasian and him an African American. I was glad they were showing everyone they didn't care about what other people thought. I will always remember that day in the restaurant when Freddy made me believe I didn't have to worry about everyone's opinion because God doesn't worry about what you are. He's concerned about what you do!

SIXTY ONE

TWENTY MINUTES after Freddy left the apartment, someone knocked on the door. "Who is it?" I said, wondering who knew I lived in the building beside Freddy and Trixie.

"It's me Trixie," said the voice.

I opened the door. Trixie looked like a New York City cab driver, with a hat known as an "Apple-Jack," and a pencil behind his ear. He also wore a dashiki and dungaree pants.

"We've got a problem," he said sounding worried.

"Come inside," I said looking over his shoulder to see if anyone was following him. "What's up?"

"Muhammad called me about an hour ago and said David Cross came by his house and started asking questions."

"What kind of questions?"

"If someone pretending to work for the Immigration Department came to see him."

"What did he tell David?"

"That no one came to see him, but Muhammad said he knew the detective was looking for you."

"How did he know that?"

"Because David described you perfectly and I'm wondering if this asshole knows where you live?"

Trixie's question about him possibly knowing where my apartment was started me thinking. Something told me I should have known him, and his father were bound to catch on sooner or later, since me and Freddy weren't professionals. The question now was, what were Phillip and his son going to do?

"What's the matter?" Trixie said, noticing the look on my face.

"Nothing, but I think I'm going to stay here all night, so me and Freddy can clean up all this stuff tomorrow just in case David does know about this apartment."

"You want me to give you a hand?"

"No," I said quickly. "I don't want anyone to know about you just in case he does show up."

"I appreciate that," Trixie said gratefully. "And one more thing I want to tell you, Mr. Sherlock Holmes. I'm really proud of you for what you did to help Muhammad, and everyone else."

"Thanks for driving me around while I took those pictures."

"You are very welcome, sweetie."

Trixie left the apartment. I walked into the bedroom hoping me and Freddy would be able to get everything in the apartment packed and ready to go by tomorrow evening.

SIXTY TWO

I WOKE UP TO THE SOUND of the telephone ringing on the night table beside my bed and picked up the receiver. "Hello," I said yawning.

"I figured you might be there," Freddy said on the other end. "Your mother said you ain't been home all night and to tell you to call her if I did find out where you were."

"We may have a problem, Freddy."

"What kind of problem?"

I told Freddy what Trixie said and that we needed to pack everything just in case David came around with a search warrant. Freddy said he would be right over.

"Where are you now?" I asked.

"At a hotel on seventh avenue with Katheryn. I told her about us going undercover and she was really pissed about me not saying something a long time ago."

"So, everything is all right?"

"Yeah, and I told her no matter what kind of baby we have, we're still gonna name it after you."

"What do you mean?"

"If it's a girl we'll call her, Thomasina. And if it's a boy we'll name him, Thomas."

"You're crazy," I said grinning. "I'm going to run to the store and buy some food. In the meantime, pick up some boxes so we can pack this stuff."

"Okay, I'll see you in about thirty minutes."

I was still wearing my grey sweatsuit and basketball shoes when I fell asleep and decided to just wash my face before going to the store. There were bottles of chemicals on the bathroom floor I used to develop the pictures and rolls of film hanging like rope from the ceiling over the bathtub. I splashed some water over my face and rushed out of the apartment. The Jewish Delicatessen on the corner of Broadway by the subway station at ninety sixth Street was crowded with customers. It took over thirty minutes to get two orders of salami and cheese on rye bread and a half gallon of milk to go.

As soon as I reached the apartment door, I heard a gunshot and put the groceries down by the staircase. I opened the door with my key and came face to face with David Cross holding a revolver in his hand and standing a few feet away from Freddy. Freddy was lying on the living room floor with his right hand over his shoulder and curled up like a baby.

"FREDDY!" I screamed, running over and kneeling beside him.

Freddy's eyes were closed, but he was still conscious. His face was extremely pale, while he held his hand over his left shoulder where he had been shot. I pulled his hand away to look at the bullet wound. The shell had gone straight through the upper part of his arm and appeared to be just a flesh wound. I took off my sweatshirt, bawled it up, and pressed it against his shoulder to help stop the bleeding. Freddy started groaning. Tears streamed down my face while I placed his hand over my shirt to keep the pressure on his injury. "Hold on, Freddy, hold on," I said crying. "I'm going to call an ambulance."

I stood up and looked at David. He was wearing a blue sports coat, grey pants, and a white shirt. "Why did you shoot him?" I said raging with anger.

"Because he was resisting arrest."

"Resisting arrest?" I said, staring at the gun in his hand. "Why was he being arrested?"

"For impersonating someone from the Immigration Department,

just like you did," he stated harshly. "Did you really think my father and I wouldn't find out about the two of you snooping around and asking people a lot of questions about us? What were you thinking anyway?"

"We're going to put you and your father in prison for blackmailing people, that's what we were thinking smart ass," I said with my hands on my hips. "And we have the stuff to prove it."

David laughed. "Let me tell you something you little queer, that's not going to happen because my father happens to be a very smart man," he began arrogantly. "And let me tell you something else. I know all about your mother and that her real name is Fatima Muttalib. I also know that she and your father are wanted by the Arab Government for killing two Muslim Soldiers. So, if anyone is going to prison, it will be them."

I started walking towards David to use the telephone in the bedroom. David pointed his revolver at me. "Where do you think you're going?" he said pulling the hammer back.

"To call an ambulance," I said and kept walking.

"Stop right there, or you'll get shot too," he said angrily.

I didn't think David would shoot me since I was a police officer. I remember hearing a gunshot and feeling a sharp pain go through my stomach, but all I could do was throw my arms around David's neck to keep from falling and then scratch his face with my fingernails as I collapsed to the floor.

SIXTY THREE

THERE WAS A KNOCK AT THE DOOR. "Come in," said Rosemary.

The secretary poked her head inside the chambers. "Phillip Cross and his son are here, Your Honor," she said politely.

"Send them in," said Rosemary while sitting on the couch with the Sergeant.

The secretary walked away, but left the door open. Phillip Cross was the first to enter. He was dressed the same as he was at the subway station. David Cross had the same beige suit, striped tie, and cordovan shoes he wore earlier. David closed the door. Rosemary left the couch and stood beside her desk.

"Why don't the both of you have a seat?" she said pointing to the sofa.

"I would prefer to stand, if you don't mind?" said Phillip cordially. "Hopefully this meeting won't take very long because I have another appointment after this."

"I thought you told my father Thomas was going to be here?" said David with both hands inside his pants pockets.

"How did you find out my wife and I are wanted for murder?" said the Sergeant looking at David.

"Why don't you ask my father, he's the one who found out before I did."

Everyone glanced at Phillip Cross.

"Your wife told me she was having trouble getting out of the country with her son, so I had David get her another passport, but the embassy told me two soldiers from the Ottoman Empire were killed and they had pictures of you, Fatima, and the real Rosemary Shumsky at some church in Antioch. They said Fatima shot Rosemary accidently, based upon eyewitnesses at the place where the soldiers were killed."

"That's a goddamn lie!" stated the Sergeant.

"Be that as it may, you and Fatima Muttalib are wanted for murder," he said looking at Rosemary.

"Listen Rosemary, or Fatima, let's cut to the chase. The Arabs wants you for murder and the U.S. Government might want to know about me and my son getting a little extra money from a few immigrants over the years. You tell on me, I tell on you, and we all get arrested. Only me and David will just get a slap on the wrist, while you and Robert go to prison in a country that may execute you and your husband."

"Listen, smart ass, David is going to prison for murder, and you're going right along with him for being an accomplice," said the Sergeant rising to his feet. "My son knows everything, so you won't be going to prison just for extortion."

Phillip laughed. "Thomas is dead according to the report I read," he said smiling at his son. "Or are you expecting him to come back from the dead to testify against us?"

"For your information, he's already back, asshole," said the Sergeant folding his arms together, "and he's going to testify against the both of you."

"Well please tell me where he is, so I can get his side of the story," said Phillip impatiently.

"I'm Thomas Shumsky!" said Rosemary sitting behind the desk.

Phillip Cross and his son suddenly stared at the Sergeant's wife.

"What did you say?" said Phillip perplexed.

"I said, I'm Thomas Shumsky. And just so you know it's true, I'll tell you something that happened at Chi Chi's Birthday party because no one else was inside the V.I.P. Room but six people including me."

Rosemary told Phillip Cross about him and his son being in the room with a gay boy named Ricky Munoz and a woman dressed in a black negligee named Jasmine Boris. Then she described how Phillip was dressed, what his son was wearing, and the satin dress worn by Chi Chi Quintana. Rosemary folded her arms together and began to describe the V.I.P. Room perfectly, along with the fact that two bottles of bourbon were on the wooden coffee table with marijuana cigarettes in the ash tray. She also mentioned beating up Clarence the bodyguard because he forcibly tried to put Trixie out of the night club for reasons that she wanted to use the lady's room, and he wouldn't allow it because she wasn't really a female.

Phillip Cross was stymied. He knew it was literally impossible for someone to return from their grave. Nevertheless, Thomas was alive again, he thought. What really baffled him was how Thomas Shumsky was able to come back from the dead as his own mother!

After unfolding her arms, Rosemary transfixed her eyes on David Cross. "I have the pictures of you taking money from the immigrants, so your father's career is over," she stated, "and you're going to prison because you lied on the report and said that I was shot while standing at the door, but the scar on your face came from my fingernails, so I couldn't have been at the door like you said."

Phillip looked at his son. "What is she talking about, David?" he said still amazed. "You told me Thomas was killed accidently?"

"She's lying, Dad," said David removing his hands from his pockets. "Frederick Steinberg and I were wrestling with the gun, and it went off and shot Thomas while he stood at the door just like I said in the report."

The Sergeant stuck his hands into his pants pockets as if he were impersonating David. "Let me tell you what's wrong with the report you wrote," began the Sergeant. "First of all, Frederick's blood was all over my son's sweatshirt because Thomas took it off to help stop the bleeding where Frederick had been shot. Which means you shot Frederick first. But you didn't think about it when you put the shirt back on Thomas and dragged his body to the apartment door to make it look like he was shot at the door."

The judge's chamber became as quiet as a cemetery.

"And..." the Sergeant continued with his indictment, "the coroner said the skin under Tommy's fingernails belong to a Caucasian, which means he scratched your face right after you shot him at close range, so Thomas couldn't have been by the door like your report says."

David reached inside his jacket and withdrew a 32-snub nose from his holster. "Sit down," he insisted while aiming the revolver at the Sergeant.

"David, put that gun away," said Phillip Cross alarmed. "You're in enough trouble already."

"Listen Dad, these people are lying," said David as if he had been convicted by a jury. "If we let them get away with this, we'll go to prison."

"Nevertheless, we'll get an attorney and do things the right way," returned Phillip sympathetically.

"We don't need a lawyer, we need to let the Arab Government know about them, since they're the real murderers."

Phillip walked towards his son. "You need to put that gun away before someone gets hurt," he cautioned.

As David watched his father walk towards him, he tried to keep an eye on the Sergeant and didn't notice Rosemary tiptoeing in his direction. David suddenly realized she was headed towards him. Rosemary attempted to kick the gun out of his hand from where she stood. David tried to shoot Rosemary, but the force of her kick caused his hand to fly upwards as he pulled the trigger. The gun erupted. The bullet ricocheted off the ceiling and struck Phillip Cross on the top of his head! Phillip collapsed to the floor. David stared at his father. Rosemary jumped in the air and kicked David in the chest. David fell backwards and hit the floor with the gun still in his hand. The Sergeant instantly removed the pistol from his holster." Put that gun down," demanded the Sergeant, pointing his weapon at David.

Rosemary rushed towards Phillip and knelt beside him. She pressed her ear against his chest. Phillip's heart wasn't beating. "He's dead!" she said looking at David.

"LOOK WHAT YOU'VE DONE," exclaimed David. "YOU MADE ME SHOOT MY OWN FATHER!"

"Put that gun down, David," repeated the Sergeant. "I'm not going to tell you again."

"Give me your gun, David," begged Rosemary holding out her hand.

David glanced back and forth at Rosemary and the Sergeant. "I don't know how you know so much about what happened, but it doesn't matter anymore does it?" he said distraught. "Thomas is dead, my sister's boyfriend is dead, and now I've killed my own father. So, what else could happen?"

David pointed the gun towards his temple.

"David, what are you doing? Please give me the gun," said Rosemary continuing to hold out her hand. "Think about what you're doing."

"I've already thought about it," he said pulling back the hammer. "You just make sure those Arabs don't catch you and your husband, Mrs. Shumsky."

"David, I'm ordering you to put that goddamn gun down right now," reiterated the Sergeant.

David smiled as he pressed the barrel against the side of his head. "You know something, Mrs. Shumsky. I really liked your son ever since we were in high school," he said with sincerity. "I just wished he would have liked me half as much as he did Frederick. Which is really why I shot Frederick."

"But trying to take my money with Billy Blocker when Freddy stopped you that day in school, wasn't the way to show me how much you liked me," she said stubbornly.

"You really are alive again," he said astonished. "How did you do it?"

"I don't know," she replied truthfully. "All I know is God wanted me to come back and prove my death wasn't accidental."

David shook his head as if he believed his own death was what God wanted now. "Pray for me, Thomas," he said frightened. "Maybe God will have mercy on me the way he did you."

"DAVID, WAIT…," yelled Rosemary rising to her feet.

The gun in David's hand discharged again. The blood from his skull splattered across the shelves of law books against the wall by the door. David lay on the floor a few feet away from his father with the revolver in his hand. The Sergeant was completely stunned as he lowered his weapon and gape at the two dead bodies stretched out on the floor.

The secretary came bursting through the door. "Judge Shumsky, are you all right?" she asked, surveying the office.

"Yes, I'm fine," replied Rosemary completely startled herself. "Call the hospital and let them know there's been an accident here, would you?"

"Yes, ma'am, right away," said the secretary rushing out the door.

Rosemary turned to the Sergeant. "What in the hell just happened, Dad?" she said looking numb.

The Sergeant returned his revolver back into the holster, not knowing what to say. Rosemary stepped over the two dead bodies, walked up to the Sergeant, and threw her arms around his neck "Listen Dad, I don't know how long this spirit stuff is going to last, so I want you to promise me something."

"What's that?"

"Don't forget what you said about adopting some more kids when you and mom start over and what you would do if one of them happens to be like me."

"I won't forget," he grinned.

"Take care, Dad, and just remember if God does let gay people go to Heaven, I'll be looking down on you and mom every now and then just to see how you're doing."

"You be sure and do that, Tommy," choked the Sergeant with tears in his eyes.

Rosemary suddenly fainted in the Sergeant's arms. The Sergeant lifted Rosemary up, placed her on the couch, and took off the tennis shoes. A few moments later, Fatima Muttalib opened her eyes and sat up on her elbows. She instantly noticed Phillip Cross and his son lying on the floor together.

"What in heaven's name happened to Phillip Cross and David?"

"What do you think about us adopting some more children?" he said, folding his arms together.

(TOBECONTINUED)